ANGRY YOUNG MAN

"LYNCH DRILLS TO THE QUICK . . . . IT RINGS TRUE."—*BOOKLIST*

CHRIS LYNCH

AUTHOR OF THE NATIONAL BOOK AWARD FINALIST *INEXCUSABLE*

Critical acclaim for *Inexcusable*

★"Lynch has hit a home run with this provocative, important read."

—*Kirkus Reviews*, starred review

★"Through expertly drawn, subtle, every-guy details, Lynch creates a nuanced, wholly believable character that will leave many readers shaking with recognition. . . . Unforgettable."

—*Booklist*, starred review

"*Inexcusable* is a not-to-be-missed chapter in the anthropology of ritual male dating behavior. From the first phrase to the last phrase, Chris Lynch creates a character with such flawless self-deception that the reader mistakes being seduced with being stalked. In the end you become the book's trophy, and you'll find your head mounted on the cover."

—Jack Gantos, author of *Dead End in Norvelt*, a Newberry Award–winning book

"Chris Lynch is the best pure YA writer we have—he has the guts, he has the chops, and like his readers, he'll take a close look at anything. *Inexcusable* is irresistible, in its limning of the spaces between brutality and grace, between the soul and the law. Start at page one—you'll never stop."

—Bruce Brooks, author of *The Moves Make the Man*, a Newbery Honor Book

"This raw and powerful book will hammer its way into your heart and haunt you. The world needs this story. And you want to read it—trust me."

—Laurie Halse Anderson, author of *Speak*, a Printz Honor Book

Critical acclaim for *Angry Young Man*

★"For those who wonder about the roots of homegrown terror and extremism, National Book Award Finalist Lynch pushes the spotlight from the individual to society in a story that can be brutal and ugly, yet isn't devoid of hope." —*Publishers Weekly*, starred review

★"The story is well paced and provides an eerie look into the small town of repressed aggression in which the boys grew up. . . . A quick read, but one that will stay with readers long after it's over." —*School Library Journal*, starred review

"Lynch cuts to the quick during this short novel. . . . It rings true." —*Booklist*

"Lynch creates in Xan and Robert a set of truly complex characters; there are no angels or devils here, just a pair of young men on the brink of adulthood who can't quite grasp the autonomy each craves and needs. Lynch continues to be an edgy yet compassionate spokesman for working-class kids, respecting the dignity of modest aspirations even while critiquing the ethical shortcomings of his characters." —*BCCB*

Critical acclaim for *Kill Switch*

★"Lynch's writing, parched with desert-dry humor, is so fine that a breakfast table conversation is just as gripping as the paranoia-laced scenes of the trio evading a shadowy doom. A compact, frayed-nerves bundle of brilliance." —*Booklist*, starred review

"A great premise, developed with brilliant prose. . . . Characters are sympathetically and vividly evoked, and the brief novel is a model of good writing." —*The Horn Book*

"A psychological exploration that leaves readers with just as many interesting questions as answers." —*School Library Journal*

ALSO BY CHRIS LYNCH

Inexcusable

Kill Switch

ANGRY YOUNG MAN

CHRIS LYNCH

SIMON & SCHUSTER BFYR

New York London Toronto Sydney New Delhi

SIMON & SCHUSTER BFYR

An imprint of Simon & Schuster Children's Publishing Division
1230 Avenue of the Americas, New York, New York 10020

For information about special discounts for bulk purchases, please contact Simon &
Schuster Special Sales at 1-866-506-1949 or business@simonandschuster.com.
The Simon & Schuster Speakers Bureau can bring authors to your live event. For more
information or to book an event, contact the Simon & Schuster Speakers Bureau at
1-866-248-3049 or visit our website at www.simonspeakers.com.
Also available in a SIMON & SCHUSTER BFYR hardcover edition
Book design by Krista Vossen
The text for this book is set in Berthold Garamond.
Manufactured in the United States of America
First SIMON & SCHUSTER BFYR paperback edition August 2012
2 4 6 8 10 9 7 5 3 1
The Library of Congress has cataloged the hardcover edition as follows:
Library of Congress Cataloging-in-Publication Data
Lynch, Chris.
Angry young man / Chris Lynch. – 1st ed.
p. cm.
Summary: Eighteen-year-old Robert tries to help his half-brother Xan, a seventeen-
year-old misfit, to make better choices as he becomes increasingly attracted to a variety
of protesters, anarchists, and the like.
ISBN 978-0-689-84790-5 (hardcover)
[1. Brothers—Fiction. 2. Conduct of life—Fiction. 3. Protest movements—Fiction.
4. Single-parent families—Fiction. 5. Mothers and sons—Fiction.] I. Title.
PZ7.L979739Ang 2011
[Fic]—dc22
2009052832
ISBN 978-1-4424-5419-4 (pbk)
ISBN 978-1-4424-1989-6 (eBook)

ANGRY YOUNG MAN

THE SWEEPER AND THE STRIKER

I want you to understand my brother. I don't *need* you to, so don't get all worked up over it or anything. Ultimately you can do what you like. But I would like for you to understand him.

As far as that goes, I'd like to understand him myself.

"What are you doing with those on?" I ask him when I walk into the room. He is just standing there, unoccupied as he often seems to be, in the small bedroom we still share. It's about three years after we should have stopped sharing a room, or much of anything else, but this is beyond our control. The *those* I am talking about are tinted glasses, kind of dark amber, which make him look something like a 1970s pimp. "They make you look like a pimp."

"Don't talk to me like that. You know I don't like that kind of talk. Anyway, they are glasses. I wear glasses, to be able to see, and you know that."

I do know that. "I didn't know that you wear pimp glasses, though. You wear them to see hookers, is that it? Can I have a shot?"

"Did I ask you to stop talking to me like that?"

"Like what?"

"Like . . . *stop it*, Robert. I'm serious."

He is. He is very serious. My brother has a number of problems, one of them being me. I am a pain in his ass, and I know it. He is also very fortunate to have me, and he knows it.

Our combined age is thirty-five. I am one year older, and this room is not big enough for all this accumulation of guy, but it is the only room we have for the moment. There is another room here, and that belongs to Ma. It's a very close, warm, and intimate arrangement. It could drive you nuts.

"They're too dark, anyway," I tell him.

"They are for my sensitivity to light. The eye doctor prescribed them special for my sensitivity."

The more serious he gets about something, the stronger my urge to laugh. I realize this is not helpful, but oh, well.

"I don't see how glasses are supposed to stop you from crying every time you watch *Titanic*, Alexander."

"I do not—"

"You also do not have a sensitivity to light."

He pauses, composing his argument. "You are not a doctor."

"Point taken," I say, and pause to compose my counter-argument. My counterargument is a penetrating I-know-you-better smile. "Now, why the tints?"

Because I am me and he is him, surrender is inevitable. "They're for privacy."

"What kind of privacy?"

"I'm shading out my windows. You know? The eyes are the windows to the soul? Well, I am tired of people staring in, trying to see my soul. People look in and think they know you, think they have you. They steal pieces of you that way. So, I'm blocking out access to my soul windows."

I have to credit him this much—it's pretty effective shading. Because the lenses are nearly the exact light caramel color of his eyes, there is a subtle camouflage effect that seems almost like you can stare right *through* his eyes, but not into them. As if you were looking straight through to the back of his scary skull. Eerie, but effective.

I won't be giving him credit, though.

"Who would want to steal pieces of you? That's like robbing a landfill. Why bother?"

I cannot help it. I have tried to stop, but since we were way small, teasing my brother has been a kind of narcotic that I can't quit, giving me a vague sense of well-being even when I overdo it a little bit.

"Don't you have someplace to go?" he asks, pretending to be disinterested in me rather than livid.

"Hey," I say, "that's my line." It is my line. Because I usually do have someplace constructive to go, while he does not. I have a job, and I am part-time at the community college, aiming for full-time. I play soccer for the local men's team, and I have a girlfriend. None of these things applies to Alexander, and it is a hobby of mine to point this out.

"As a matter of fact, Alexander, I had this hour set aside for a little downtime, to rest up in peace for the busy evening ahead."

"Robert, I asked you not to call me that. Can you just respect me enough to call me by my preferred name? Can you just manage to work up that small bit of respect for me and do that much? It's not a lot to ask, is it?"

What he prefers to be called is Xan. He has become attached to the notion of it because of its more exotic ring. I have pointed out to him that Alexander the Great was both Macedonian *and* great—pretty exotic without sounding mental—but this fact has not impressed him at all.

"Sorry, Al," I say.

I know. I have to do better. They say that excessive reddening of the face does not indicate high blood pressure—after causing it so many times, I eventually felt obligated to look this up—but I am not convinced. His head looks like a really big sandwich bag being pumped up with cranberry juice.

"Jesus, Xan, calm down already. It'll just take some getting used to. You did pick the most awkward of all your syllables. Cripes."

You'd think that would pacify him, right?

"Don't blaspheme, Robert," he says. "You know that bothers me."

"It didn't used to bother you."

"Yes, well, disgusting vile pork rinds never used to bother me either—"

"Hey," I snap, "don't blaspheme pork rinds. You know how that bothers me."

"Robert," he says, nostrils slightly aflare, "while I have not yet found a religion that speaks to me on a personal level, I have concluded it is right to treat everyone's faith with respect. I would think you could—"

"Pork rinds," I say.

"What?"

"They are my religion. Pork rinds. Please show respect."

"I hate you," he says.

"Of course you do," I say, brushing past him to flop onto my bed. "You hate everybody."

He doesn't. Hate me, that is. I'm not so sure about everybody else, though.

"You coming to the game tonight?" I ask him as he stretches out on his own bed.

"I don't know," he says, followed almost without pause by, "I suppose."

He never misses my games. He loves me. In spite of everything. I don't know how he manages it, really. I'd hate my guts if I were him. He's got a good soul hiding behind those windows.

We are walking together, Xan and me, to the park, which is only a few blocks away. Walking with him is great—it aids communication. When he is standing still, he always looks trapped and desperate, like he'll make a break for it at any second. He likes to walk, though, and sometimes to run. That sense of getting somewhere, even if it's somewhere modest like White Stadium—which is not much more than a grass field, so that the "stadium" bit is a mystery—makes him a better guy to talk to. Because he can feel a little less like a ne'er-do-well. Which, he kind of is, really.

"How's it looking for a job, Xan?" I ask as matter-of-factly as I can.

He stops short, right there on the corner. His brakes practically screech.

"Jeez, it was just a question," I say.

"No," he says, waving me down, "shush."

I see that he's not bothered about me at all. I follow his intense focus out into the street, to the other side, where a line of funeral cars is passing, headed toward the crematorium.

"What are you doing?" I ask.

"Trying to make eye contact," he says.

"With . . . a funeral?"

He does appear to be doing just that. His eyes, just discernible in the pimp glasses, travel right to left with the hearse, then jump to the flower car and follow it several yards, then jump to the next and next cars.

"Stop that," I say, putting my hand right up and deliberately smudging his glasses. "What's the matter with you? People don't want you doing that. Why are you doing that?"

He is wiping down the glasses with a special little chamois he keeps in his pocket.

"To connect, Robert," he says simply. "I do it all the time."

I tug on his shirt, and we continue walking. "You are a serious freak, Alexander. Does anybody ever look back? Like intense, like the way you were doing?"

"Sometimes, yes. Those are great moments, when that happens."

I look sideways at him to be sure he is not pulling my leg, which of course he isn't, because he is Alexander, but he deserves the look anyway.

"Xan, you haven't made a new live friend since you were, like, seven, and now it's important to you to *connect* with grieving, mobile strangers?"

He waits a bit, presumably translating his thoughts into something I can comprehend.

"People need to connect, especially at hard times," he says. "I'm trying to be helpful."

See, he says these things. He says these things and he makes me see that his intentions are good even if his GPS is set for the planet Blurg. But while he is making me see this, I have to gently try to make him see what everybody else sees.

"Stop staring at funerals, ya maniac. You really need more constructive uses for your time. Which is why you are lucky to have me. Watching me excel at soccer will be constructive for you."

He makes a *hurnn* noise, signaling that he has not exactly seen the light, but we are soon at the field, and now he is kicking a ball back and forth with his big brother, which, I can see right away, is good for him. It's always good for him.

He wasn't bad when he played at school. Wasn't as good as me, but wasn't bad at all, at school. He wasn't bad at academics, either, when he tried. Wasn't as good as me, but wasn't bad. He never should have quit either one.

"You never should have quit," I say when he sends a nice little backward-spiral chip shot that lands softly right under my foot. I flip the ball up and play a bit of keepie-uppie.

"I never quit. They forced me off the team," he says, watching me with his hands on his hips.

"They never did," I say, popping the ball up, left foot, left, right, left.

"They did. Stop hogging the ball."

I flip the ball up and pop it his way. He begins playing keepie-uppie. He was always pretty good at this. Not as good as me, but pretty good.

"Xan, requesting that you attend classes and achieve some level of grade results is not the same as forcing you off the team."

He's doing all right. Six, seven, eight . . .

"Hey, how many of those can you still do?"

As soon as I have asked, there is trouble. Maybe he wasn't counting, and now the effort of digitizing in his head is interfering with the physical performance. As if the god of coordination instantaneously withdrew his gift, Xan shanks the ball off the side of his foot and stands staring angrily at me as it squibs away.

"I'm guessing from your expression that you are blaming me for that," I say.

"Only because you did it on purpose, Robert. It's what you do, after all."

Unfortunately, this makes me laugh out loud. "Okay, if I over-complicated things, how 'bout I count for you while you keep the ball up next time?"

He is walking in the direction of the ball. "I never even said I wanted to know how many I could do," he snaps—in my opinion, comically. "I was happy there, just enjoying doing it. You were the one who needed to put a number on it, just so you could top it, of course, by multiples of ten or something. Jerk."

The coach has beaten my brother to the ball, scooped it up, and is walking toward him with it. "Is he being a jerk?" the coach asks.

"Yes," Xan says.

"Yeah, sweepers tend to be jerks. It's kind of in the job description. And he's a powerful sweeper. Therefore—"

"A powerful jerk!" Xan says excitedly, as if he's gotten a really difficult quiz answer rather than the most obvious one. At least he appears to be making a friend.

"Stuart," the coach says, putting his hand out.

"Xan," my brother says, accepting the challenge.

It is unusual, for both of them, to do any unnecessary mingling. Even when he is in a mood to kick around with me pregame, my brother always manages to scamper away by the time anyone else joins us. And the coach tends to be too busy, preoccupied with sustaining the team's mediocrity, to notice anything on the periphery. Unless he's looking for something.

"You seem to know what you're doing with a soccer ball," Stuart says.

I walk up close so the three of us form a cozy huddle. "He was very good in high school, Stu. Until he quit because he got tired of hearing how he was no me and he never would be."

"I never heard that," Xan protests vigorously. "Not once did I ever hear that."

"Maybe you didn't hear it, but they were saying it."

"Hey," Stu intervenes, "if you ever hear it around here, Xan, 'You're no Robert' is a good thing."

Alexander does something he does not do often enough. He smiles. And this, believe it or not, makes me smile. I am sure it looks like we are now competing at some freakish smiling contest.

"So, you want to play with us?" Stu asks my brother.

His smile slides away, as he himself nearly does. He takes a

couple of instinctive steps backward. "Oh, thank you, but . . .
I don't know. . . ."

"We could really use you, Dan."

"Xan."

"Xan. Honestly, we are kind of shorthanded this evening."
Stuart gestures toward an unimposing collection of casuals kicking balls randomly in the distance. We're not exactly a power-
house at full strength, even in our modest little league. With
numbers down, times will be tough. "You look like you got
good wheels, and we could really use somebody up front. It'd
help us out."

"He was a striker in high school!" I say with more enthusiasm
than I would have expected, though I take not a volt of it back.
"Xan, this is great. Come on, man, you are needed. What's better
than being needed *and* playing the beautiful game on the same
team with your gifted brother?"

He is fidgeting, nervous, as awkward as hell as usual, but also a
bit excited. I have asked him twenty times to give this a go, but
the coach stepping in has clearly tipped things. "Well . . . I've got
some things to do."

"What, funeral-bothering? Come on, man."

"I don't even have any gear—"

That is all we need to hear. Stu and I each grab one of Xan's
arms and we all jog over to the collection of kit bags and guys
stretching, and in no time at all my brother is in shorts and
cleats and is reintroducing his hamstrings to the exquisite torture that is warming up for the first time in more than a year.

"Ahh, ahh," he says with an almost crack to his voice. He is
lying on his back while I hold his right heel and push it in the

direction of his head. I won't even say how much fun it is on my end, because that is irrelevant and this is a job that must be done, but I do not take my eyes off the carnival of muscle twitch and fracture that is Xan's face. Suddenly his eyes go way wide in a different way entirely as he looks right past my shoulder and his foot.

"I don't believe what I am seeing."

The voice belongs to my girlfriend, Babette, and so my eyes go wide with excitement too. I let go of my brother's leg and let it snap to the wet turf like in a big mousetrap. I pirouette to give her a squeeze.

"Isn't this something," she says.

"Yes, it is. I didn't think you were coming," I say.

She's not even paying attention to me, I don't think.

"Xan, you're playing with these guys. That's great," she says, giving me a little shove and standing over him.

For his part, Alexander lies mostly motionless where I dropped him. His legs aren't moving at all, but his grin is electric, and his eyes are nearly burning through the silly brown lenses of his glasses.

"I can't feel my leg," he says, about as cheerily as a person could say that.

I go to him, and give him a hand up. "It's been a while, that's all," I say. "Give the blood a chance to circulate back around in there."

He limps around, bouncing, kicking, giving it a bit of a hokey-pokey shake here and there. Then he's off on his test lap.

"This is a very good thing," Babette says when he breaks into a jog around the field. "This is just the kind of thing he needs."

"I know," I say, and before I have a chance to say anything else, like how wonderful it was of me to arrange it, or that's the kind of guy I am, Babette emphatically addresses the subject of the kind of guy I am.

"Make sure you make him feel a part of the team," she says.

"Ouch, ouch, ouch," I say. This is less because of my hurt feelings and more because of my hurt sternum. Babette has fingernails like gardening tools. Especially the index emphasis finger.

"Okay," I say. "Of course."

"Not, 'of course.' For you, 'of course' would mean prodding him like some hapless lab monkey until he went berserk in front of the rest of the team, all in good fun."

"Well, it *would* be—ouch. Okay. Anyway, I wouldn't do that. You don't really think I'm like that."

"Yes, I do."

"Not in front of other people. I wind him up, Babette, but not the serious stuff in front of other people." And at this moment I am truly wounded, on the inside. "He's *my* lab monkey."

She desists from the poking just short of reaching my literal physical heart. But she completes her point all the same. "I don't think you do it all on purpose. But you need to be more aware. He's not like you, Robert. He has feelings. He doesn't think everything's a laugh. And I don't think he bounces back very well."

What I do here is, I remain quiet, which is my surrender.

She accepts my terms. "Good," she says, leaning close to my face.

Alexander has now done his lap and trotted up by my shoulder. He stands there in his signature style—awkwardly.

Spontaneously Babette lunges over and grabs him in a great, tight neck hug.

It could be strangulation—Babette is a take-the-breath-away hug machine—but I know my brother, and the redness bubbling up from his neck to his hair follicles is the sweeter shade of bashful.

"Now, let's see some soccer, boys," she says.

We both turn to join the rest of the team warming up, but Xan is way ahead of me already, bolting like he did as a boy, as he hasn't since he was a boy.

MAGIC SKEWS

We are not full brothers. We have different fathers. Not that it even shows, or matters. We look like full brothers. You might even think our mother is lying when she says we have different fathers, though why would she bother?

She is a wonderful woman, Ma. With absolutely abysmal crap taste in men.

She is single currently. Which is probably just as well.

Alexander has never met his father. Lucky Alexander.

The man who is technically my father—or as Ma now calls him, "the Slime Donor, SD for short"—came to dinner one time. I was about twelve, and didn't even know who the guy was until we were half done eating. When Ma had a man over, Xan and I were usually pretty who-cares about it as long as we still got to control the TV and the guy didn't linger too long over breakfast.

"My *what?*" I said, mashed potatoes still nesting in my gaping mouth. Bless her, she was trying to spring him as a surprise, like dessert in the middle of the meal.

"Your father," Ma said calmly, making the subtle *Close-your-mouth flapping* motion, with her fingers flicking her chin.

"Our *what?*" Alexander said, letting his mouth hang likewise open, but having the good form to block it with his hand.

"No, not yours, sweetheart," she said to him. "Robert's."

"May I be excused?" Alexander asked.

She has always been a stickler for these kinds of niceties. Dinner, together, at the table, not in front of the TV. And you don't ever leave that table without first asking to be excused. When he was little, Xan always said it quick and slurred, so it sounded like "magic skews." He may actually have thought those were the words.

"Alexander, you know we always have dinner as a family," she said.

"Right," he said. "That's why I thought I would leave you alone. So you could be family."

He has always been dramatic.

"Hey," the SD said, reaching across to pat Xan's shoulder, "I might be your daddy too. Can't be sure, right?"

I saw my mother cringe just there. Like the food was producing some wicked stomach cramp. As the old man laughed at his cleverness, I leaned close to my brother and whispered, "You can have him. I don't mind." Which made Alexander laugh even harder than "Dad."

Poor Ma. I don't know how she'd expected this to go, but it

wasn't going well. First SD embarrassed her at her own table. Then her sons perpetrated first-degree rudeness by whispering at the table and then laughing at somebody.

Laughing, at not just any somebody.

"Sorry, Ma," I said when I saw the fracture zizz across her face. "Sorry, sir," I said then, to our guest.

He gave me a slant smile and squint that somehow communicated to me right away, *Not as sorry as you're gonna be if there's any more of that, wise guy.*

And he was right about that.

Ma and Alexander were left washing the dishes together while me and ol' Dad went for a walk to get dessert.

"How much you got on ya?" he asked before we had even rounded the corner.

I looked sideways, to see what I could see. "How much what?" I asked.

He laughed. It was a jolly and friendly, though not fatherly, laugh. "Call me Dad," he said.

I was feeling very fast-tracked here, and not at all sure how I felt about it, and not at all sure what I could do about it. After all, this was, my father?

"How much what . . . Dad?" I said.

I had dreamed about that, about calling somebody that. This lean and stubbled face had not been in the dream, however. Still.

"Dough. Money. The dinner guest isn't expected to buy his own dessert, is he?"

Is he? How would I know? Where was a guy like me supposed to get information like that?

"Dad?" I said, and nope, it didn't slide out any easier. I dug into my pocket and flat-palmed him my findings, which came to maybe two bucks, maybe three in silver left from my leaflet money. I had shoved a lot of leaflets through a lot of mail slots for that money. Got my fingers snapped quite a few times too.

He scooped it right out of my hand, cupped it, and shook it like maracas at his ear. "Well, we won't be getting fat on sweets tonight anyway."

He was still laughing when Xan's voice came calling from behind. He was running, half breathless by the time he caught up. He ran right to . . . the guy, and stuck some bills in his happy agreeable hand.

"Ma said you forgot this," Xan said, completely flat, neutral, like he didn't even know what the papers were that he was handing over.

Some weeks I made more on my leaflet route than Ma made waitressing. She does better these days. But not better enough for this move.

"Well, that's a little more better," he said.

Xan didn't even say another word before hotfooting it back to Ma.

"He's a bit squirrelly, that guy," the man said.

"Duty bound," is what I said back.

"Huh?"

Ma may not have approved, but she wasn't there, and this was between men, and anyway it was just right to ask then, "What is your name?"

He squinted a less friendly version of his ready smile at me. "Wayne," he said.

"Duty bound, Wayne. That's just the way my brother is."

"Half brother."

"My *brother* has a sense of duty the way a lion has a sense of meat. He's running back because he has not finished helping my mother with the cleaning up, and that kind of thing matters to him."

Wayne looked off in the direction of Alexander. "Like I said, squirrelly."

Dessert turned out to be a box of Ho Hos, two liters of Dr Pepper, and a cigar that smelled like a petting zoo on fire.

I broke yet another rule of manners as we sat there again at the table. I stared. And stared and stared and stared, at Wayne, who was supposed to be my father. The shock of meeting him, after wondering about him for years, was surprisingly short lived. It was as if my mind, somewhere deep where I could not see it, was processing and filtering the man way ahead of what my conscious and conscientious mind was capable of. But the result was, he had checked in and checked out of my life almost simultaneously, and I was sure that my ability to sort out men was natural and sharp in exactly the way my mother's was not.

I would have given anything at all to be able to transfer that skill to her.

She didn't scold me for staring at Wayne, because she spent most of the evening staring at him herself. It was a different kind of staring, one that liked the raunchy cigar smell and the deep, smutty-sounding laughter at almost everything he himself said. She was lonely. I knew that, because she talked to me about it, talked to both of us because we were her best friends. But only now did I realize how lonely lonely was, if this was better than not having a partner. Myself, I'd rather have been alone.

Alexander fell somewhere in the middle. He took this father thing, this appearance or audition or whatever it was, seriously. He was the one of us most invited to opt out, since he was the only one with no connection to Wayne at all, but he was also the one with the most curiosity about the situation.

"Are you going to live here now?" Xan asked out of nowhere. That was a conversation grinder.

"Why would you ask me that?" Wayne said, turning—not happily—away from my mother's ear. "Don't you like Ho Hos?"

"I love Ho Hos," Xan said calmly. "Are you moving in here? With us? Are we moving in somewhere with you?"

You might say Alexander was a young eleven, and you might be right. You would be even more right to say he was an unusual, and unusually direct, eleven. His policy about information was always that if he wanted some, he asked for it. That remains his policy.

"Alexander!" Ma said snappishly. "Don't be embarrassing."

Ma was surely embarrassed by the turn in the conversation. Wayne was irritated. Me, I was sick to my stomach.

I looked down to be sure that I had not lost track and eaten all the Ho Hos and washed them down with all the Dr Pepper, and had punched myself in the abdomen. I hadn't. I had in fact taken only one small bite, one small sip, and set it all aside. I felt like puking because of the power of suggestion, of Xan's suggestion, that we might all live together.

"I'm sorry," Alexander said. "I didn't mean to be embarrassing. I just wondered."

"That's okay," Wayne said, drawing hard and wafting a cloud of cigar smoke to hover perfectly over the table among all of us.

"Why don't we just take it a little slow. Hell, your mother hasn't even asked me yet."

Ma laughed and slapped Wayne's arm, my stomach churned like a washing machine, but Alexander just nodded thoughtfully, like just accumulating more details for his file.

Wayne lasted a week. We never actually saw him again after that dinner, but we could hear him, hear them, when he showed up at night, a little later each night. The walls were thin, the nights were long, and the sounds lived with Xan and me, floating in the air above our beds like that toxic awful smoke from his cigar. The sounds of joy, which were bad enough, were followed by sounds of conflict, followed by sounds of joy again. By the end of the week, it had all been pretty completely replaced by the sounds of fear and anger and disgust and sadness and hate, until it was all replaced by the thrilling sound of total nighttime silence.

But the Ma of the days, of the mornings for a long time after that, was the Ma of disappointment and loneliness beyond what she had been before. She smoked in the mornings then, at the breakfast table, instead of eating.

"Is he not coming back, ever?" Alexander asked on the second day of cigarettes.

"You shouldn't be so gullible," I said, walking angrily away from perfectly scrambled eggs that had a fleck of ash in them.

"Who are you talking to?" Xan asked.

I wasn't sure.

"Don't breathe on my food, Robert. I mean it," Alexander says, defending his plate with as much of his body as he can get on the table without actually lying on it.

If you breathe in close proximity to his food, he cannot bring himself to eat it. I almost never do it anymore, but he still acts as if it's a constant battle.

I slap him on the back as I pass by. I pose no threat to his food.

"I really don't think I like those glasses on you, Alexander," Ma says. She is at the head of our three-by-five-foot teak veneer table, while the brothers sit, as always, across from each other. She insists still that we do something like a formal dinner every night. Maintains the family unit, she says. It is kind of sweetsie, kind of desperate, and perfectly all right with both me and Alexander.

"They guard his soul windows," I say in a way that makes it obvious I find this humorous.

"What?" Ma says, tilting her head as she regards him more closely.

"I swear, Robert, I will just take my plate and eat out on the curb if you start."

"You will do no such thing," she says.

"The windows to his soul," I say to her. "Alexander is afraid the world is peeping at his exposed soul. So he is camouflaging it."

"So, let them peep," she says. "You have a beautiful soul, Son, and should be proud to show it to the world."

Xan sighs deeply and angles his head so he is staring directly into his food.

"What happens if you yourself breathe on the food?" I ask him. "Does that count? Does Ma have to cook all over again now?"

"May I be excused?" Xan asks Ma's perfectly cooked boneless hyper-garlic fried chicken.

"No. Robert, stop winding your brother up. Alexander, pick your handsome head up where I can see it."

I stop. He picks his handsome head up. She smiles. He cannot help smiling back. Being predominantly human myself, I join them.

The truth, not that he would ever tell me the truth about it, is that he is hiding his eyes because they are big soft softy eyes. He wants to show the world a hard face, but, frankly, he hasn't got one.

"I think hiding your eyes at the table is like wearing a hat at the table, or coming to the table with no shirt on," I say helpfully. "Ma, I think you should insist that Alexander bring his eyes to the table when we are all here eating together nice like this."

He is glaring at me now across the table. It is mostly glasses, but I know what's behind them, and I can also see gold bolt flashes of lightning in there.

"Robert is just being a pest," she says, "but I do think that is a valid point, Alexander. I would really love to be able to see you when I am sitting with you. You don't really need the glasses for eating, and if you do, you can get your old clear ones instead."

It is a beautiful and complex thing, their relationship. Blood and thunder, fury and respect and disapproval and upheaval and unconditional love, but with stipulations. And I know he cannot put up resistance to her in a case like this.

He is like a bull snorting as he stares down into his food for several more seconds. Then, before raising his head, the glasses are removed, neatly folded, placed beside his plate.

"Ah," I say with joy that sounds like mockery but is really laced with a lot of affection, "there's our boy now."

Ma speaks not, but her face is in total agreement with me.

"You'll just never understand," he says to me with some anger, and those famous soft eyes filling up wet.

It's about our fathers.

Having never seen his father, and with Ma always refusing to discuss the man, Xan has been left the leeway to create. He has created an outsider.

"It's easy for you, All-American Eyes," he says to me, not for the first time. "People look at you, and it's all apple pie, and Vote for Robert. People don't look at me like that, and you know it."

I know nothing of the kind. What I know is that the only substantive difference in our looks is the eye color, yes, with mine being the color of honeydew melon, and his being somewhere between butterscotch and caramel. Soft and sweet in both cases, one will note.

"Xan, the only thing people see in your eyes that they don't see in mine is delusion."

"It's true, though, you are more Caucasian than I am. Nothing personal, Robert."

"Okay. One, you are talking about my *person*, so how can it not be *personal*? Do you know what the word 'personal' actually means? Two, are you suggesting that I should be *personally* offended at looking either more or less Caucasian than you? And three, you look exactly as Caucasian as me, Alexander. That is just going to have to be one more cross for you to bear."

"You know what it's like for me, Robert? It's like going through customs, all day long."

"You don't even have a passport! How would you know that?"

He shakes his head sagely, like he pities me. "You'll just never get it, will you?"

"Well, cripes. Whatever it is, I *hope* I never get it. Is it contagious?"

RED MIST

Coaches wield a great deal of power. Not in just the obvious ways in the obvious situations like being the coach of the New England Patriots gives you power. Far down the scale, and in subtler ways.

Even the coach of a podunk neighborhood team in a podunk league can pack a certain kind of power for good, and you wonder if they realize that. You hope they do.

"I am really glad to see you back," Stuart says, shaking my brother's hand again as if one or both of them is running for podunk local office. "You showed me a lot last time out, especially with it being your first game of organized ball in . . . How long was it?"

Alexander is beaming.

Trust me that that bears repeating.

Alexander is beaming.

"A year, I guess. Maybe a year and a half. It depends on what your definition of organized is, actually."

"Dammit, boy, that is promising," Stu says.

Alexander shrugs.

"Guess you haven't had time to get some proper sports eyewear," Stu says suggestively.

"I had time," my brother says. "These are fine now."

Stu looks to me. My turn to shrug. He shrugs back.

Alexander is adjusting the strap that now holds his glasses to his face. It's not a real strap you would get for pennies at a drug store, because that would be too straightforward and mainstream for my brother. It is a makeshift thing he worked up from an elasticized band he sliced out of the bottom of one of his sweatpants legs. He said he didn't like the tight-at-the-ankle style of sweats anyway, but, being Alexander, he now has one leg that way instead of two. At least his specs won't slide down his face the whole game.

Which is what they did last time. Slid down his face, up his face, crosswise across his face, and clear off his face. Toward the end of the game he was running basically nonstop with his index finger placed just so at the bridge of his nose to keep it right. It was quite a trick, kind of cute, mental.

And he still played *well*.

Even I didn't recall him being quite as good as he was. The boy's got wheels, no doubt about it. Despite his lack of match-fitness, he kept up with every sprinter on the field. He maintained his position, got open regularly, passed crisply even if sometimes it was to nobody in particular. He ran hard for the net every time we got near scoring position and never dogged it getting back when we were defending.

It wasn't quite fluid, working him into a team that has been practicing months together, but it wasn't as sloppy as you might expect, either. Could have helped if he'd communicated a bit more, but he's not one of your natural shouties on a field. It'll come.

He got two shots, and came close to scoring. One he just missed over the crossbar, and another was barely saved by a magical dive from their six-six freak of a goalkeeper. Both times, though, Alexander came running back upfield as if he had put a game winner in the back of the net.

It was the support, wasn't it? Yes, you'd have to say it was the support.

The guys playing up front were clapping for him, shouting him into position when he was unsure, calling his name like they had known him as long as me. The coach was bellowing like a sea lion on both misses, telling Xan he was nothing but unlucky and his chance was coming. Babette uncurled such a quality scream on both near misses, I swear I got an erection, and I was certainly not the only one.

The boy was light-headed with the praise. He looked like he could run forever, at top speed.

Until it was over.

Adrenaline depletion, I believe they call it. We stopped at a coffee shop halfway home. Xan hates coffee, but he insisted. After we sat down, I knew why.

He laid his head down on the table, iced mocha in front of

him. He had his arms folded and his face to the side, like they have you do on your desk in the earliest years of school. He could have been five, right there, as I watched the top of his tired head.

"Pretty fun, huh?" I said, sipping my own mocha through the fat straw. We had lost the game 3–2, but that was two goals closer than we had been to winning yet. "And you, you were a Robostriker, man. Where'd you get all that gas?"

He paused as if to figure out where he had gotten it from. Then he inhaled deeply, ramping up to produce an answer. Then he exhaled, and inhaled, in that old familiar way I knew meant he was sleeping. Just like that.

Just like that. That was how Alexander got back into soccer, and not too soon either. He is stretching now, and adjusting his homemade glasses strap. He gets to his feet, starts bouncing up and down on the high school cleats he pulled out of retirement, adjusting the shin guards that came along with them. He bounces some more, testing the security of the glasses, though I think he would bounce right now without any purpose at all.

"You'll want to consider getting some proper sports goggles, like the coach suggested," I say.

"These are perfectly functional," he says.

"Sports ones will be better. This isn't high school anymore, Xan. And we play a lot of games around dusk. When we get one of those dark gold sunsets, your eyes and your lenses and the horizon are all going to be almost the same color some evenings. That can't be good for contrast and spherical object recognition."

"These are fine," he insists. He's even talking like Robostriker.

"If I'm not going to let regular people see into my soul windows, I'm sure not going to let the opposing team look in, now, am I?"

He bounces a couple more times, then bursts into his wind sprints without waiting for anything like an answer. Good, since I don't have anything like an answer.

When the game gets under way, I sense something different about Alexander's approach from early on. It isn't that he isn't putting the energy in like last time. He may be pushing it even harder. In fact, that is it, that he is pushing it even harder.

The first ten minutes of the game are possibly the fastest, fiercest ten of soccer I have ever been a part of. It is moving at the speed of ice hockey, on a small rink. The team we are playing is good, a lot better than the last team we played. They are skilled enough but not dazzling. The thing they are known for is toughness. They are conditioned, and relentless, and, famously, unconcerned with what anybody thinks.

We got hammered by them last season. They stopped counting the goals after halftime.

But we are playing them toe-to-toe for the first ten minutes. We are as fast as them and as sharp and as rugged, and the main difference, I have to say, is my brother.

"Pace yourself," I shout as Xan runs madly up the right wing, waving his arms for our center midfielder to get him the ball. The pass would be too long, and he's not open enough. The guy passes left instead, and that player passes to the midfielder coming through the middle, but the shot goes mental, about ten feet over the net.

Xan runs back to position as hard as he ran to the net. I yell his name, catch his eye. I make the *Slow down* motion with both hands, like a traffic cop. He shows no sign of acknowledgment.

The ball is back to me a minute later, center of the park about twenty yards in front of our goalie. Two of their forwards are at me like peregrine falcons at a pigeon, but I split them and smack a clearing kick well downfield. I am watching to see if Xan beats their defender to it, when I find myself thumping, face to the ground, with a mouth full of turf.

That's the game. It's what they do. Ref makes about a sawbuck for the game, so he's not really going to sweat an in-depth investigation, is he?

I am on my elbows checking the play when I see Xan gesturing madly with his hands and screaming in this direction. He stopped pursuing the ball when I went down. He is screaming at the ref.

"Play on!" I hear Stuart holler from the bench.

Too right.

"Play on, Xan!" I scream. "Play the ball! Play to the whistle!"

He continues screaming as the action flies past him in this direction, and before I can even clean gritty dirt and coarse grass from my teeth, they are with me again. The same two falcons are bearing down, having passed their way by the other defenders. One more pass, right past me, and the one guy is free on the far side, heading goalward.

If I may be a little immodest here, this is my thing.

I chug, like a train. I go from zero to sixty in two seconds, do not think finesse or ball possession or manners. I have one aim, and I aim for it.

Chug-chug-chug-chug-chug-chug-BOOM!

I come across that field so fast and explode on the striker so hard, he actually yelps with shock and awe. He never thought I'd be back in that play, and he never thought he'd be sitting on his sore ass watching that ball sail away out of the park and into the nearby neighborhood like a fifty-yard NFL field goal.

It is the most satisfying part of my job. I love being a sweeper.

The crowd on our side of the field erupts as if we have won the World Cup. It is deafening, but that is what fans do. My team mostly claps and shouts encouragement, keeping an appropriate cap to the celebration so early in such a tough game.

Except one teammate.

Alexander hollers and jumps so maniacally, everyone has to look. I give him the *Calm down* hands again, and guys closer by go up and have a word.

The best result of that big-boy sweeper intimidation clear-out is that you get their attention. You get them thinking twice for the rest of the game, looking over their shoulders, worrying about my defense instead of their offense.

The worst result is, you piss them *right* off.

Like I said, this was never a roll-over team.

By the twelfth minute the glorious first ten of our performance is just about a memory. The score is 2–0 to the bad guys, and it becomes clear they intend to get even badder. I am defending a corner kick, lined up, bumping forwards as per my job description, when the nipping starts.

"Aw," I snap. "Jeez." I throw a discreet elbow into the guy's solar plexus, but the ref whips his head in my direction at the sound of the guy's yowl. I won't be getting away with something that blatant and effective again. The nipping, on the other hand . . .

He gets his thumb nail and index nail together, like a pair of nail clippers, and *nip*. Cripes, it stings. He nips my back. My side. My back again. I would rather be punched in the head than nipped. Just as the ball is about to be kicked, I step backward and stomp the guy's foot.

And he punches me in the back of the head. Better.

Worse, though, he follows through the punch by grabbing the back of my shirt as he launches himself into the air. He times it perfectly, and heads the ball right into the top of the net.

Their team celebrates, my team yaps at the ref, and we all march back to positions to start it all over again.

"What's going on here?" Xan demands as we walk up a few yards together.

"Just play," I say. "Ignore all the nonsense."

"We should kill these guys."

"Don't kill anybody, Brother. Just play the game as well as you can."

His head is all red, with exertion and indignation.

"And pace yourself," I say.

He jogs to position, but I can see him, staring at opposing players who are especially egregious. I see him point and gesture and pay all the wrong kind of attention.

We take the ball out, midfield pushing up, moving the ball to the forwards crisply. Nice pass out to Xan, who spins, takes on a defender, and loses the ball to a good tackle. Trying valiantly to get back into the play, Xan chases the guy down, reaches in slightly, and flicks the ball away.

It is a borderline play. There may have been minor incidental contact, but honestly the play was fine enough that Alexander should have gotten the call.

The other guy, though, flies through the air as if Xan attacked him in full lacrosse gear. He sails through the air, hands outstretched, mouth open huge like some manga kid, and screams as he hits the ground. The ground, by the way, is pudding soft after three rain days.

"What?" Xan screams as the ref blows his whistle and marches toward him with a yellow card in the air. He starts screaming a lot more than "what" as he enters a state of high agitation.

Our two other forwards rush ahead and wrap Xan up before he can do any more damage.

Damage, I fear, has already been done. I can tell by the way Alexander is sort of pacing in place before play resumes that things are in motion within him. And the other team can see it too.

Play resumes, for about thirty seconds, before it gets worse. They are leading by six goals, and we have not hit halftime yet. The other guys drop into their old tricks and spend as much time antagonizing our players as trying to score. They hack without mercy. They nip with the dedication of a team of lobsters. And they whine and dive like the Italian national team.

"What is wrong with you?" Alexander screams, standing over yet another playacting forward crying on the ground. He is apoplectic with rage that the guy is putting this much effort into the crap fakery part of the game.

He is right, of course.

But that means nothing.

Xan actually drops to his knees to berate the guy, until the ref comes over and insists he get out of the way. Xan screams at the ref. Then he screams at the team medical guy who comes to help the poor helpless hapless cheating jerkwad by spraying something, probably a nice cologne, onto his boo-boo ankle.

People on both teams are starting to laugh at my brother's sincere outrage. It is kind of comical to watch.

Unless you know better.

I can see him from our very different positions on the field. And even though I can see mostly only my brother's tense and heaving back from the distance, I can see his mania.

Now I remember why he stopped playing this beautiful game.

We take the ball out after yet another goal is conceded. Pass, pass, rush, not bad, not any obvious surrender. Courage, boys. Character, good.

Then we lose the ball once more, to a neat and fair slide tackle by one of their midfielders who collects the ball and starts a rush.

Alexander, from his spot way up the wing, starts chugging, like a train, like his big brother. I can see him clearly because I am backpedaling, keeping the play in front of me. The player, the ball, coming right my way. But not as fast as Xan is.

He's chugging like me, more brute force than finesse. Of course I recognize it. Part of me is quite flattered. Another part of me is quite concerned. Not really part of his job description, the way it is mine.

The ballcarrier is going mid-speed, and he is right in front of the ref. He cuts into the center, taking one of our midfielders with him, pivots shockingly, and blows past the guy as he cuts back outside. He is running toward the sideline, right toward the ref, just as Xan catches up to the play, with a full head of steam. Major steam.

"Hey," Alexander yells at the last instant, catching the ball-carrier's eye.

I don't even know what sport to compare it to. The impact has definitely got some hockey, some football, with maybe a little cage fighting thrown in. But definitely not soccer. When Xan hits the guy, he dips the shoulder perfectly. He rams the guy in the right pectoral, just enough off center to make him spin away from the crash with the whip of a tetherball at the end of a point.

I can hear both thumps from thirty yards. The thump of guy on guy, and the thump of guy on ground.

The other player is howling. He was already his team's chief crybaby, but this is new.

Xan stands over him glowering.

The guy's really howling.

"I'll *give* you something to cry about," my brother says.

The ref had the best seat in the house for this. He is right up in Xan's chest now, with a red card held high for all to see.

Xan glares at the ref and points down at the writhing victim on the ground.

"Now, *that's* a foul," Xan says.

THE DRIFT

In our league an ejection earns you an automatic suspension for two weeks. To contemplate what you have done.

"I didn't do anything," Alexander says.

Not a great start to the contemplation.

"It's soccer, man, not Ultimate Fighting Championships."

"He deserved it."

"He did, indeed. Just like you deserve your suspension."

"Come on, Robert. A guy has to draw the line someplace, doesn't he? Did you see that team? When they weren't hacking, they were flopping. They went back and forth from assaulting us to crying like babies. They were so . . . *RRRRR!* I am getting steamed up again just thinking about it. It ain't right, Robert. It ain't right."

"Contemptible."

"*That's* the word. Thank you."

The right word at the right time helps you make sense of the world. It helps, but sometimes not a lot.

"Even if they were one thing or the other, y'know? Thugs or crybabies. At least that I could understand a little bit. At least that is just, well, you gotta be what you gotta be, after all. But to be both? God, that makes me *so* angry. . . ."

"Yes," I say, rather foolishly laughing. "I can see that."

My brother has possessed a highly developed sense of outrage for as long as I can remember. Once, in high school, at lunch I ate my carrot cake before eating my chicken à la king, and he moved to another table.

"Listen, my brother, I am on your side. I know where you are coming from. You are a destructive force, yet you are a righteous destructive force. But the fact of the matter is, you have to take your medicine for this, so just take it. Do your two weeks and come back to the team fresh and focused and motivated like we need you to be."

He pauses, a good whole minute.

"I was really enjoying it, Robert. I have to tell you, I was really, really enjoying playing, being on the team and all that. Felt good."

"Good. Great. So, hold on to that feeling, and come back stronger. Oh, and saner. Come back stronger and saner."

He pauses again, nearly as long. It's almost as if every time I mention the suspension and the time lapse, he is thrown once more. As if by talking to me he is going to maybe make the outcome different.

"It's a long time, Robert. I'm not even allowed to come near the team, not for practices or anything."

"League rules. They've had some colorful discipline problems, and had to get ultra-tough or lose city field permits."

"What will I do?"

"Jeez, Xan, you were only on the team for two games. Find something else to fill the time for a while. And get a job, dammit."

"I've been trying. You know that."

"Try harder. And spend the time working out. Burn up some of that nuts energy before somebody gets hurt. Before you know it, you'll be back with the team, and you'll be a force to be reckoned with."

The pauses, though still with us, are at least getting shorter.

"I have a really serious question to ask you, Robert."

"Okay."

"Do you ever get the feeling like you want to kill a guy? Actually, for real, kill him?"

You would have to say this qualifies as a serious question. I take it in, slow it down.

"Well, Brother," I say, "like every other sentient being, I have to answer, yes. Yes, I do. Pretty much every day. I've killed a couple, even, but they weren't popular people, so it was okay."

He just stares. He needs you here, Rob. Come on.

"Okay. But the answer is still yes. I do think about it. Sometimes I don't know. If I could get away with it, would my behavior be different? But things are not different. And so, what keeps guys like you and me as functioning and free-ranging members of civilization is a certain amount of self-control. We have to be able to manage at least that. Alexander."

He stares.

"I do wish you would stop with the staring right now, as, what with the topic and all, it's a bit unsettling. But I'm making a wild guess that you think about killing folk. I think as long as you keep it in the playground of your mind, you're okay. And don't let it take up too much space, even in your fantasy world. If murder supersedes humping in your dreamscape, I'd say that is a pretty effective definition of insanity."

Now he just looks disgusted. "Do you have to bring everything down to that level?"

"*Down?* I thought I was elevating the discussion."

He waves off my philosophy, and returns to his more immediate problem.

"I miss the team," he says.

I nod—sagely, if I'm not mistaken. "Put it to use, man. That's the best advice I can give you."

To my surprise Alexander follows my advice. He is up early, out for long runs. He's got my dumbbells in his hands nearly every time I see him. He is going after jobs, researching at the library, applying online, in person. He runs again before dinner, and after dinner he is even taking an interest in televised sports for the first time since junior year of high school. I believe we have turned a corner with the boy.

"You should see him, Stu," I say to the coach when I get back to practice. "I tell you, he's a new man. He's working out like nobody's business, and I think he's really going to show you something when he gets back."

Stuart looks less enthusiastic than I had hoped. He looks down, then off over my shoulder, toward the rest of the team running sprints and stretching. He tosses a ball back and forth between his hands, then calls out for Marco, who's our team captain.

"What?" I say to Stuart when it's clear something is wrong.

"I'm afraid he's not going to show us something when he gets back, Rob," Stuart says.

"Why not?"

Marco trots up behind me, pats my back in a friendly way. Always liked Marco. He's a good choice for captain. Control is what Marco is all about, as a center midfielder, and as a guy. "Hey, Robert," he says, "how you doing?"

"Okay, Marco."

"It's just," Stuart resumes, "we got all our guys back now. Everybody's healthy. . . . It's a numbers game. We really have no room for your brother at this time. Maybe next season, if he comes in at the start . . ."

"He doesn't really fit the game plan, Robert," Marco says.

"The game plan?" I snap. "What is the game plan, then? Losing? We lose almost all the time. Maybe it's time for a new game plan, guys. My brother can *play*."

"I believe he can," Marco says, nodding earnestly.

"Absolutely," Stuart agrees. "The boy's got wheels, for sure, and a nose for the goal. . . ."

"I wouldn't want to have to cover him," Marco says.

"No," I say, thinking like now we are getting someplace. "Exactly. Who would want to cover him? Nobody, that's who."

"Problem is, Rob," Stuart says, placing a fatherly and ominous paw on my shoulder, "nobody really wants to play *with* him either."

Maybe because he's my brother, I never saw it coming. I was prepared to answer but was not prepared *with* an answer, so my mouth just hangs there open. I look to Marco.

"Like coach says, Robert, maybe we bring him in beginning of next season, see if we can work with him. Right now . . . he's really raw, kind of out of control."

I stare at Marco.

"Nobody wants to play with him? Marco?"

He looks at Stuart, then over his shoulder to where the guys are pretending to play but are paying more sly attention to us. Then back to me. "Coach is maybe overstating it a little bit . . . but, yeah, it's not a good fit right now."

I should be better on my feet than this, but I am not.

"But he's my brother," I say.

I seem to share with my brother a gift for making these guys uncomfortable, because there is a great deal of shifting going on. Marco takes the ball from Stuart and starts rotating it in his hands. Stuart claps his hands together and starts rubbing.

"Like we say," Stuart repeats, "maybe next year. If we integrate him early . . ."

He may be finishing that sentence, and Marco may be contributing something else cheering and meaningless as I grab up my bag and head on home.

I give it the full two weeks before I tell him. Does that sound rotten? I haven't been able to decide. The first night I rolled over about three hundred times, trying to get a comfortable sleeping position, one where the thoughts about Xan getting dumped from the team would drain out of my head rather than banking up in there. I kept kicking and rolling until the man himself made me cut it out.

"Robert, come on. I have to get up in the morning. You should quit with those stupid energy drinks all day, man. Those things are poison."

He's right, I should quit them. But they were not the problem— that night, or the next one, or the next. *Look at him,* I thought, *he's running, he's pumping, he's focused. He's even got rosy cheeks, I swear he does.* I wanted to string this out as long as possible, hoping the benefits he'd gain over two weeks would give him momentum, and give him the strength to overcome the knock of getting shoved off the team. Those were real, and real good, reasons not to tell him right away.

Not as good as fear, though. I have to admit that I was afraid to tell him.

What would it do to him? I had seen into those soul windows, all the way in, but even I did not know the depth of how sensitive Alexander really was, is.

It sucks to be dumped—whoever you are and whatever you are dumped from, even if you really didn't want that particular situation anymore anyway. Even if you were pretending that you didn't want that situation anyway. Even if you were strong and resilient and had other offers out there waiting. Even if those things were true, it sucks. It hurts.

And if you were Alexander?

"It's a numbers game, man," I say as he stands there with his kit bag dangling from his grip. That is how late I let this go. He's standing there, in front of me, like a little kid with his bag all ready to go. The first of the players so deeply offended by my brother would be arriving at practice right about now.

"Numbers," he echoes numbly.

"Everybody who was out—hurt or whatever—they are all back and available now, so there's just no room on the squad. They know you're good, though. They said maybe if you want to try next—"

"Where's your bag," he says like a zombie of an ex–soccer player.

"I don't know," I say impatiently. "What difference does it make?"

"You're going to be late for practice," he says.

"Oh. Right. I'm not—"

"Suddenly they had no room for you, either? Is that what you're going to try to tell me now?"

I have to smile, just a little bit.

"I'm going to try, yes," I say.

"Mmm," he says, dropping the bag there at his feet. "That makes sense. You're only, like, amazing as a sweeper and probably the best player on every team you've ever played for. Why would they have room for that, right?"

"It's a brutal world out there, Brother. A brutal game."

"Robert, don't quit your team for me," he says. He sits on his bed and unlaces his shoes. He stands up and changes as we talk.

"I'm too busy, Xan, and that's the truth. I don't really have time for the team right now, with work and school and all."

"Honestly," he says, pulling up his shorts, "I wasn't even going to play much longer myself. I couldn't stand to play in that league of yours, with all the diving and the hacking . . . makes me sick, to be honest. There's no—"

"'Honor' is what you're thinking, Alexander."

He pulls on his T-shirt and emerges pointing a gun finger at me.

"'Honor' is what I'm thinking, Robert. There's none."

The good thing is that he is going out for a run. Like he has done the last several evenings at about this time. Just like nothing ever happened.

Just like nothing ever happened.

The whole apartment quakes when he slams the big metal door behind him.

I cannot tell you what Alexander does with all the time he has. It has always been something of a mystery to me, outside of the brief and idyllic time of his soccer career. And intensive inquiry is not only fruitless but dangerous.

He kept up the working out for another week or so, tapering off, running hard whenever he received another form rejection to another job application, then not running again until he had a good, angry reason.

I think, over the last year, he's been walking a lot. Like, he leaves the house and . . . walks, for large chunks of days.

"So?" Babette says as we walk along the street, holding hands. "Do you really need to know? He's getting space for himself. It's a small apartment, and he lives squashed up against the likes of you. Is it any wonder he needs a lot of fresh air?"

I tug her hand and bring her up close for a captive hug.

"How would *you* like to live squashed up against the likes of me?" I ask.

"You are such a romantic, Robert. But let's take it slowly, huh?"

It is a nonsense suggestion anyway. Babette and I met at the community college, where we are both still students and where we are headed right now. We have very little time for such romantic nonsense, and even less money.

But, so what?

"Come on," I moan, holding tight to her right there in the middle of the sidewalk with no intention of letting her go. "Listen, it makes total sense. You and I can study together, so that's like combining both our studies into one, reducing our study time by fifty percent. That frees up a lot of sex time and *still* allows time for you to take on another job. And think how happy Alexander will be with his own room."

"I'd like that," Xan says, startling us both as he steps onto the curb from the street.

"Jesus, Xan," I say.

"Blaspheme?" he says, wagging a *No-no* finger at me.

There is a guy standing next to him.

"This is Bobbo and Babbo," Alexander says by way of bogus introduction to his friend.

"Harry," the friend says, offering me a firm handshake like a bag of rocks. "Nice to meet you, Bobbo."

"Robert," I correct him as Babette bursts out laughing. Alexander smiles boyishly. He loves when she laughs. "That's enough out of you, Babbo," I add.

"Doesn't bother me," she says, offering Harry her hand. "I think it's cute. In fact, we should use that from now on."

"Great," I growl.

Xan grins even wider.

"Happy, are you?" I ask.

"So this is what it feels like to act like you. I guess I can see the attraction."

"Where are you two off to?" Babette asks.

"The college," Xan says, and we all start moving in that direction.

"*My* college?" I ask.

Babette and I are walking arm in arm, behind Alexander and Harry. As he walks, Xan keeps looking over at his pal, and up, since Harry's about three inches taller. Harry is a rugged, solid-looking guy, with about the coolest Fu Manchu mustache I have ever seen. Xan bounces along a little excitedly beside him, clearly in admiration. The way he used to do with me a long time ago.

"Harry has invited me to come and sit in on a class he's taking, Social Responsibility."

Something in the air here is causing me to bristle. I can't be this easy to replace, can I? And when I bristle, I get kind of big-brotherly, in the snappish way.

"You can't just stroll into somebody's class, Xan," I say. "It's a college, you know."

"He can in this class," Harry says without looking around. "In fact, it's encouraged. The instructor says the more people who come to this class, the more successful the class is by definition."

Alexander turns a victorious smile on me, then looks ahead again. Babette squeezes my arm and tugs, a similar message.

I don't like this.

"I don't like this," I whisper in her ear.

"Jealous," she whispers back.

I do not dignify it. Maybe she's right. I mean, she isn't, but maybe. I watch as the four of us head to the school. I watch as my brother watches Harry, and I see the stark contrast that I am betting Xan does not see. I see Alexander's soft, eager, and wounded eyes, and I see in Harry the kind of strength and self-confidence my brother is looking for.

Harry is the kind of hard-man Alexander wishes he was.

We approach the gleaming glass front of the newly built main building of the CC. It is a clean and airy front to a building designed to attract all comers from the side of town we call home. The semester is only a few weeks old, but it is my second year here, same as Babette. We have both been happy here, feeling like we belong, like we are accomplishing something, getting somewhere. That's what we are supposed to feel, so I guess they are doing a good job.

I wonder, as Xan and Harry walk together down the big wide corridor, if the college will be able to have the same success with Alexander. That would be good. That would be a really good thing.

This college has already succeeded where nobody else has. He's through the door.

"No," Babette says, snapping me out of my staring trance after my brother. "That's just stupid."

I turn to her. "What is?"

"Your plan. For sex and study and cohabitation. We can't condense time with buddy-study if I'm studying ecotourism while you're studying sports coaching and development, now, can we?"

I am back to staring down the hallway, even though the guys have slipped into whatever class they are socially activating in.

"Bette, what do you think of him?" I ask.

"Who?"

"Harry."

"Oh, him. Well, I think he's damn cute, there, Bobbo. That's what I think."

"Yeah," I say absently. "Yes, right."

"Well," she says. "That statement was designed to get *you* all insecure, not me. That didn't work out at all."

"Nah," I say, reassuring her. "Nah, don't worry about it. It'll work out fine, I'm sure it will."

After a pause she does her elongated "Ooooh-kaayyy," which signals that something not quite right has come out of me. She kisses my cheek and shoves off, literally. "Get to class. See you right here afterward."

THE GOOD CAUSES

My mother does not cry, you understand. Not ever. I have never seen it, and enough evidence has accumulated that I never expect to.

I walk up the outside stairwell that squares around our big squat rock of an apartment building. It's a nice night, like most late-September nights are nice, and though it has been a long day, the air is clear and I am enjoying its crispness as I mount the steps. I get to the third and top landing, make my way down to our molded metal door, and stick my key in.

I work days, go to most of my classes at night, and when I find myself here addressing this lock at night, all I ask is for the tumblers to tumble.

But it feels rusty, the old lock. I have to remember to squirt some WD-40 in there, make everybody's life a little easier before autumn gets late and winter sneaks in behind, the way it always seems to do when I don't pay attention.

"I told you, I will *have it*," comes my mother's strained voice through the four-inch opening in the window a few feet away. She loves the air, especially in autumn, just like I do. The window is just off the landing where I stand, opening out over the small patch of grass below and the lined parking spaces. On the inside it's just above the little desk she keeps in the corner of the living room.

The lock is fighting more than it has in ten months. WD-40, dammit.

"Listen," she snaps, and I hear also the snap of red wine in her voice. "Listen to me. You just back off right now. There is no cause. . . . You have no right. . . . I said I will have it, and I will have it. What is thirty days to you ghouls, anyway? You'll find my blood is just as delicious a month from now."

Finally the lock pops and I burst through the door like I'm breaking and entering. Ma yelps and jumps up out of the spindly desk chair.

Alexander stands motionless, his arms folded across his chest, bloodred eyes burning orange through his tinted specs.

Ma is staring at me, one hand on her chest, breathing heavily with the fright. Her eyes, unguarded, are red rimmed. The wine goblet perched on the top of the desk explains it partly, but her wavery voice explains a little bit more.

"Excuse me, Robert, while I finish this call," she says.

She turns, calmly presses the off button, then puts down the phone. Hard, and repeatedly, she bangs the cordless into its holder.

"Who do you owe money to?"

"Go fish," she says, waving away some invisible fly with one hand and grabbing up a fast-disappearing wine with the other. That's her favorite exclamation, Go fish. "It's nothing, just the remains of some old credit card bill I forgot about."

"Credit card bill? I didn't even know you had a credit card. I thought you didn't believe in credit."

"Well, I don't anymore."

Alexander and I both follow her to the kitchen area, where she pours another half glass of wine.

"What are you doing?" Xan asks, a little harshly. "What are you doing getting yourself in such a situation where a guy like that can be calling up here and pushing you around? I don't like it. I don't like it at all."

Clearly he does not. His body language is all agitation as he vents against both sides, my mother and her tormentors.

"What are you talking about?" she snaps back. "What would you know about this situation, or any situation, for that matter? At least I work . . ."

Uh-oh.

". . . At least I get out of bed every morning and I work quite hard, thank you, Son, and I pay the rent and the electricity and the food bills. Would you know what that is like? Your brother is going to school, and still he manages to work, and to pay me something every week to try to keep things afloat, not that it's a lot, but it helps. What is it you are doing with yourself, with your time and your potential, Alexander? Who are you to stand there and get all judgey on me?"

"Ma," I cut in at the first intake of breath, "Alexander didn't—"

"I got work," he says flatly.

The conversation, thankfully, grinds to a stop.

"What?" I say calmly. The kind of calmly that is supposed to register great surprise without spoiling everything.

"I got work," he says without emotion. "I can help now. It's not full-time or anything. But it's a start. It's something."

Ma puts her glass down on the dining table. Then she picks it up and takes a quickie slug. She walks to Xan, raising her arms. He stands there, too rigid but not fleeing, at least. She gives him a big hug.

It doesn't matter a ton what the work is, as long as he's not killing people. Even the money is not of prime importance. It's the motion. It's the little progress, the cracking of a door, the small step. And the fact that somebody was good enough to hire the boy, makes you think there may be something there.

"What is the work?" I ask while they hug away.

"Sales, like," he says, all flatness still. "Nothing big, that's for sure. Selling stuff . . . cleaning products. To people at home. Door-to-door, basically. Sometimes on the phone. A combination of both, really. But they are good, the cleaning products— quality, you know? Stuff people don't have to be forced, 'cause they really do want to buy."

"Super," Ma says, and she means it.

"That's great, Xan," I say. And I mostly mean it.

"Guy says if I'm any good at it, it could turn into more. See how it goes, he says. So, we'll see how it goes, I guess."

"He's a door-to-door salesman? *Your* brother is a door-to-door salesman?"

I am in Babette's bed, and up till now things have been going pretty well.

"'Door-to-door salesman' makes it sound so cheesy," I say.

She blows smoke toward the ceiling. It is her only serious flaw, the smoking.

"That's because it is cheesy. Unless you're Willy Loman. Then it's just fatal."

This is the unexpected dividend of quitting the soccer team. I am finding myself with small bits of extra time to spend with my girl. And I am finding I really needed it.

"Maybe I should live here," I say, rolling onto my side, scootching up close and burrowing into her neck. I can feel her throat on my face as she exhales again.

"Maybe you should just calm yourself down. My parents do come home, eventually."

I do good persistence. "No. I don't want to calm down."

She does good ignore. "I suppose maybe he'll do okay at it, and maybe then it will come to something, huh?" she says. "Some people won't get him, but we know he can be charming. If, like, thirty percent of doors don't slam in his face, that'll be good, won't it?"

"Well, that's the hope, right? It's not like he chose it over a stack of other offers, so he's making the best he can. He's trying."

"He's trying. You know what else he's trying? There's a friend of mine who's in that social responsibility class he's been auditing."

"Yes?"

"Well, I get the sense he really likes her. He's being friendly, in his Xan way. Trying to talk to her and stuff."

I actually spring right up in the bed, fold myself into the old praying posture, with the clasped hands and everything. If not for the buck nakedness, I could be right back in church. "Oh, please, Babette, if there is anything you can do there. If you can help that situation along in any way at all, that would be great. I swear to you, I fear for the good of civilization if that young man doesn't get laid soon."

She laughs, rolls over, and stubs out her cigarette. Twisting, she shows me the muscles working in her slim, toned back.

"Jeez, Robert, apply a little pressure, why dontcha."

I scootch even closer. "You mean like this?"

She elbows me almost gently. "No, like this."

We both roll onto our backs to contemplate the same ceiling. It's a better place, a better bedroom than mine, but that doesn't rule out an elaborate network of ceiling cracks. It looks like a thermal image from the sky of the Amazon and its tributaries.

"What's your friend's name?"

"Carly."

"Carly. I like that name. Do I know her?"

"Well, she says you two went out for six months junior year, but my guess is, no, you don't know her in any truly meaningful sense."

"Oh, oh, oh, oh, Carly. That Carly. Oh, oh, she was sweet. That is good, that would be nice for Alexander. Do make that happen, Babette."

"I heard you already."

"What does she have to say about the social responsibility class, anyway? Does she like it? Xan doesn't let on much, and I don't push because it's so great that he's working, sort of, *and* going to the college, sort of. . . ."

"She says it's okay."

"Okay? Is that it?"

"No. She says it's . . . feisty."

The Amazon. I am in the Amazon now, in the water there with the piranhas and crocodiles, and all is well as I swim along smelling the wet green air all around me.

"Feisty?" I repeat with trepidation. "Oh, crap."

"It's not *all* Alexander, the feistiness," she assures me.

"Oh, is it not? Have we got a percentage as to which portion of feisty my brother is contributing?"

"Not all that much, it turns out."

I say an actual "Phew." Out loud, and twice.

"No, Carly says it's sort of in the course design. They want to agitate, to provoke passion and debate. She says Xan is even kind of fun."

I turn to look at her. "Could you repeat that?"

"You heard me. Somebody used the word 'fun' in regard to your little brother. He is quite idealistic when you get down to it. I think she even used the word 'quaint.'"

"That does it, Babette. Let's drop a net on this girl and haul her home to meet my mother. She's perfect."

"And I saved the best for last. They are going on a class outing together. The instructor assigned the whole class to break into twos and fours and venture out into the volunteer sector and work a half day. Then they are to bring back their report. Alexander asked Carly to partner with him, and she said okay."

"Jeez," I say, with a fist pump, "the power of education. Where are they volunteering?"

"Animal shelter."

"Yes, yes," I say, multi-fist-pumping. "Girls and stray helpless kittens and scrappy lovable motlies—it's a can't-miss. Even for Alexander. You can relax, world, my brother is getting some."

If it looks like the Amazon, why is it so cold? The temperature plummets as Babette fixes me with cold narrow eyes.

"Is that so?" she asks, her voice low. "Is that how it works?"

"Sorry, love," I say, whispering as if whispering will in any way help. "I didn't mean anything really by that. Just that, I got a little enthusiastic . . . for my lonely brother's sake."

"Yeah?" she says. "Well, don't get all that enthusiastic for him. I don't know what you did to poor Carly back when, but nowadays she's so Christian that Jesus calls her for guidance."

Now, that's a claim to make a guy think.

"I did all that? Huh, whadya know."

"Bravo, Robert," she says. I don't believe she means it in the applause sense.

PICKLE

I'm a grease monkey's grease monkey, and it's not a half-bad life. I was lucky to get it, really, lucky to get anything around here these days, and as is often the case, my good fortune was only made possible by some other poor schlub's bad fortune.

The schlub was a good friend of mine too.

I work for Nick's Engineering. Sounds sophisticated, "engineering." It's auto repair. And it's a one-man shop.

One and a half. Actually, 1.6, since my hours amount to a little more than a half-time week. I do the low-level maintenance of the place, keeping the tools and the shop floor as clean as possible, cleaner than anybody else's garage, because Nick is a freak and damn proud of it.

I arrive at seven a.m. four days a week, and when I am done with the clean routine, I get assigned the more basic of the mechanical tasks that are the spillover, the professional crumbs off of Nick's table. He will analyze and diagnose and prioritize and do all the truly skilled jobs, while freeing up his more important talents by having me remove wheels, loosen rusted bolts, change plugs and filters and fluids and all that. It's physical, it's honest, and it keeps the workday moving briskly along. I even feel pretty useful, for if you looked at the operation, you would think there are three Nicks handling all these vehicles so smoothly, and it is my contribution that makes his magic act work.

The unlucky guy who gave this job up was my old pal Billy, Nick's nephew, built like a farm boy, tall and lean but with big ol' bones that were still no defense when his hand got crushed by this hydraulic spring compressor that can seriously sort out a spring but doesn't do any favors for the human body. I saw that hand, those bones, as I was just coming in to meet Billy for lunch and found him sitting in a grease-black chair while the two of them stared at that big strong hand that now looked the image of a colossal burnt potato pancake with ketchup.

Something in that family's blood failed to recognize either pain or sentiment, because as Billy sat there, grimacing but not making a peep, Nick shook his head a bunch and said to me, "Need a job?"

So that's the fates smiling on one guy and not another, but that is the way it works, right, and when it works for you, you have to just go for it.

"That's me, finished, Nick," I say as I try my damnedest to scrub and pumice the dirty oil out of my pores and out from under my nails at the gray stone sink.

"See ya, then," Nick says without picking his head up from deep under the hood of a hopeless silver Ford that doesn't know how lucky it is.

I step out of the perpetual-dusk garage and into some fine autumn midday sun, the kind that gets you right in the eyes. I have a twenty-minute walk home, and a couple hours for napping, eating, and showering before I have to be in class.

I certainly am tired. But it's the okay kind of tired, so that's all right. I have always loved Thursdays. Once you make Thursday, you can always hump it across the finish line no matter how low your tank is.

My legs are heavier than I expected, though, as I make my way up the stairs of my building.

"You live here?" says the serious-looking man wearing a shiny tie and sitting on the top step before my door. I always thought a guy all dressed up isn't pulling it off if he's sitting on the ground.

I say nothing. He seems like the kind of guy you're better off saying nothing to for as long as possible.

He holds a legal-looking paper in my face. "This you?"

I look briefly at the paper, then back at him. "Do I look like a Maria to you?"

"Where is Maria?"

"Who are you?" I ask, reasonably enough under the circumstances and not too aggressively.

"Who are *you*?" he anti-answers.

I know nothing about this guy. I know nothing more than that we are two men here having an exchange on more or less equal footing.

And yet. Why does it seem he is holding all the cards? And why does it seem that he knows it?

"I am Maria's proud son."

"Oh, yes," he says. "Maria Junior, that's right."

"Who are you?" I repeat.

"I have business with Maria," he says, and points to my mother's signature on this sheet that is telling me nothing but telling me in an uncomfortable way.

"Maria is not here."

"I'll wait."

"Maria will not be here for quite some time."

He smiles, like he thinks I am lying. I am lying.

"I've got time," he says.

We stay like this for three or four excruciating minutes. He is sitting on my steps, above me, while I stand on my steps, facing up to him.

"As a matter of fact," I say, "I just remembered. Maria's not due back this evening."

He smiles again. He has quite a collection of those greasy smiles. He has a silver-capped eyetooth as well. "Sounds dubious."

I shrug. "Maria's got a cell phone. As soon as I get inside, I'll phone her and double-check, but I am pretty certain now that that phone call is going to certify that she won't be coming home tonight. And these concrete steps do get very cold."

He won't stop smiling. Does he know the smile's eating me? He must. He looks like he knows every damn thing.

Finally he stands, adjusts his pants to come back up over his bit of belly. He is tall. He is meaty.

"Well, Maria, we will meet again, no doubt," he says, brushing past me on the way down the steps.

I don't flinch. He smells like he washes that suit in a rinse of perfume and black bean sauce.

"I will look forward to it," I say.

When he is good and gone, and only when he is good and gone, I relinquish my tight-ass pose and allow myself to twist down onto a step. I feel as if I did more physical work in the past ten minutes than I did the whole day up till then. I have my elbows on my knees, staring straight ahead, when my brother fills my view.

"Who was *that*?" Xan asks about the departed visitor he'd have seen fleetingly.

"Never mind that," I say. "Who is *that*?"

"This," he says like a little-kid champion at a 4-H fair, "is Pickle."

He is holding Pickle tucked into the crook of one arm, legs dangling either side of the arm, chest supported in his palm.

"Okay," I say. "Now for the big question. *What* is Pickle?"

I am not joking. Pickle has short, bristly hair all over, mottled black and brown. Tall pointed ears with almost no hair but the same color pattern. A tuft of hair straight up in the middle of the head. Skin and bones is being generous. And a face that looks like it was molded out of clay and then smushed upward with the heel of a hand before it had a chance to set dry. Pickle could well have some bat in him, but beyond that it's anybody's guess.

"Don't be a jerk, Robert."

"Alexander, for this moment, and making no promises for the future, I am not being a jerk. I am being serious. What is he? Will I guess, cat?"

He snorts. Xan, that is. "*She* is a dog. And she's wonderful."

"Wow, dog was going to be, like, my fourth guess. What is *she* doing here?"

"She lives with us now."

"Are you joking?"

"I am not. Robert, she was at the shelter, and I couldn't leave her there. It was heartbreaking. She was in this tiny cage, all depressed and lifeless. Her time limit in the shelter was coming to an end. . . . Do you know what was going to happen to her?"

"They were going to send her back to her home planet?"

"They were going to gas her. Can you believe that? I couldn't let it happen."

I am looking at this unfortunate Pickle, hanging there, still motionless, still depressed, and probably just as close to death as she was in the shelter, and I can't help thinking my brother has made a well-intentioned mistake. There is no upside to making that case, however. So I go the more obvious route.

"Ma's going to shoot you," I say.

"What? No way. Not when she sees this," he says, and thrusts Pickle in my direction until we are practically snout to snout.

From the smell she is emitting, I am not sure Xan wasn't two weeks late saving this creature from death.

"Not sure this is going to sway her," I say.

A few minutes later we are sitting at the table, drinking coffee, which Alexander is developing a fondness for, and waiting for Pickle to display signs of life. She is just lying on the linoleum, four paws spread like a smelly little kite. A bowl of water sits in front of her, next to a flat plate with some ham slices a few days past sell-by. The ham has been completely ignored, while the water got just enough attention to leave open the possibility she was merely giving her face a quick wash.

"So, who was that guy?" Alexander asks.

"Collector," I say.

He nods, unsurprised. "What kind of collector?"

"I don't think it was stamps, Xan."

"I mean, what kind of bill was he collecting?"

"I wouldn't know. He had her signature on something, though."

Ma's signature is distinctive, shaped like an ostrich's claw print.

"What are we going to do about it?" he asks.

"Talk to Ma? Pay the bill? There aren't a lot of options, are there?"

"Guess not."

Pickle makes a move. Looks like she's going to get up, reconsiders, then kind of slithers toward the ham. She gets her face up on the plate, gives the meat a little lick. Satisfied, she lets her chin rest there. She starts with periodic little slurps now, like a hot horse with a salt lick. Progress, anyway.

"How is your job going, by the way?" I ask him.

"Fine," he says. "It's work. Ask me about the animal shelter instead."

"How was the animal shelter, then?"

"A nightmare. Robert, it's an awful, awful place, and something has got to be done."

"Sheesh, Xan, what are you going to do—declare war on an animal shelter? I don't think this is the outcome the social responsibility people had in mind when they sent you there."

He gets up from the table and goes to Pickle. He scoops her

up and holds her, a little more snuggly than before, as if one or both of them needs comforting during this tale.

"It's not them, Robert. They are great people, really concerned. They're doing what they can. But god, all the poor creatures . . . confused, angry, lost. They are trapped in those cramped cages and they are pissed off or suicidal or whatever and they have no way of knowing that they are sinking their own chances of getting adopted by acting like that, so they keep not getting adopted, which makes them keep acting like that. . . . The term 'vicious circle' was made for these guys."

I don't know why I didn't see this coming. I was so excited by the Carly thing I looked right past how wrong this setup would be for Alexander's fragile and chaotic heart.

Diversion is the only hope.

"How was Carly, though," I say hopefully as he and Pickle settle in across the table from me.

"Carly? She's wonderful. She's caring, and she's lovely. Really knows animal welfare issues. Likes Jesus. A *lot*."

"So, you gonna see her again?"

"Robert, this was not a date. Will you pay attention, please? These animals, despite some people's best interests, are suffering. And this *is* what social responsibility had in mind when they sent us out." He gestures at me, inadvertently aiming Pickle at me like a threat. "A person has to do something, Brother. A person has to do something."

Right now I have to do something, which is reel him in before he gets too far out there. "First, could you stop pointing that thing at me? Second, no, I don't believe a person necessarily does."

He shakes his head, purses his lips, tenses up. Pickle remains composed. "You don't believe that. You cannot believe that. Man, it's like one big rotisserie down there. The fluffy and perky safe ones get homed pretty quickly, while the majority, the normal, faceless animals without the star quality, they go nowhere. Until they get the gas, because they have to make room for the next bunch of poor saps. Did you hear about the town in Sweden where they burn rabbits to heat the houses?"

"I never heard that, but you know—"

"It's totally true. What is wrong with people, huh? Did you know about the mink farm that's only, like, a few miles from here? It's a horror movie. And the experiments on animals, going on at our own state U? Trauma. They are testing out trauma on animals, for what purpose?"

This one just comes out. Even I don't think it's smart.

"Sounds like those Swedish rabbits would be pretty traumatized, so maybe they could just combine the two programs. Save at least some suffering, right?"

In a piece of Alexander theater that is very indicative of him, because of his anger at me, he starts squeezing Pickle, until a weak small yelp comes out of her.

"There," Xan says, taking his dog and sweeping away in disgust, "are you happy now?"

He only sweeps as far as our bedroom door when the sound of Ma battling the lock pulls him back. I hear her growling at the thing, but then she defeats it just as I'm getting up.

"Hey," I say from behind my coffee mug.

"Hey," she sighs. She plunks her big heavy bag down beside the door and treks wearily toward the kitchen area.

"You're home early," I say. "Nobody eating today?"

"Everybody's eating," she answers, "but fast, like pigs at a trough. All the running, half the hours, half the pay. Joy."

She likes her job. She waitresses, at a pretty nice place that is nicer still in the nighttime, but she is happy enough with the more modest wage of the day. But liking it doesn't mean it doesn't take a lot out of her by the end of the day, and it shows. She slouches, where normally her head and shoulders are consciously squared up to the world. And she walks like a person with two limps, so they balance each other out but still look like limps.

She pats my head in one lazy swipe as she passes me on her way to the wine. She drinks more now, the last year, year and a half. Not a lot by big drinker standards, I don't think, but more than her old hardly-touch self. Almost always red wine. I approve, myself, as I often thought in the past she should drink more.

"We had a visitor," I say as she takes up her head-of-table seat.

She exhales loudly, says nothing yet, takes a healthy sip.

"Why do you have to go straight for the wine?" Alexander says, inching back into the situation with our new little sister.

"Jeez, Alexander," I say, sharpish, "take a pill. When you have been actually working for any length of time, you will appreciate the need to relax somehow at the end of the day. Oh, no, I forgot. You don't have any interest in being relaxed."

Ma throws Xan a look, then turns back to me. I am looking right into her face for a front-seat view when the reality of unreal Pickle comes over her. Slowly she turns back up to the pair of them.

"Pickle," Xan says to her.

"Nice to meet you, Mr. Pickle."

Fooling us all with this one, she is. She has nothing against animals, but has plenty against mess and smell and expense. She has always been maniacal on the point of keeping things simple, keeping our day-to-day as uncomplicated as we could manage. It's been a good policy, airtight. I'd never have guessed a doglike thing like Pickle could have breached it.

"She's not a mister," Xan points out. "She's a miz. And why are you being so suspiciously cool about this?"

"Because," she says, "I figure I let you keep your creature, and you let me keep my wine."

Hey, that was good. She caught him flat-footed there. He wouldn't want to concede the wine, but what's he going to do?

"Hnn," he says, the way less-than-gracious losers do when they are soundly whipped.

"So, who was our visitor?" she asks in a voice that says she is unlikely to be surprised.

"Some kind of bill collector," I say. "He was on the stairs when I came home from work. He waved around some paper with your signature on it. We spent some time together. It wasn't quality time. When I finally got him to leave, it felt like there should have been some horror-villain music playing him away."

Ma's wine has done an amazing vanishing trick. I never even saw a second sip.

She says nothing about the collector. She puts her elbow up on the table, rests the side of her head against her open palm, like she does, and stares past me out the front window. This lasts maybe half a minute, during which time Alexander and I exchange glances without moving our heads. Then she snaps out of it again, wheeling around in her chair to face Xan.

"Well, go fish, then," she says, gesturing them toward her with both hands. "If she is going to be living with us, I should try to get to know her, right?"

Alexander looks genuinely thrilled at Ma's interest, and he takes it as his signal to start his animal rights rant back up again. "Did you know about the mink farm?" he asks. "Just outside town? Do you know that sometimes the minks get the fur stripped right off them while they are still alive, if they haven't died quick enough?"

"Oh, Alexander!" she says, taking Pickle in gently and holding her upside down and cradled like a baby. "That is repulsive. Do you want to give me nightmares?"

"Yes," he says, "yes I do. I want to give everybody I can nightmares about the appalling mistreatment of animals in this country."

"Goodness, she's awfully spindly," Ma says, stroking the soft belly of the upturned dog. "There is hardly anything to her at all. And she's trembling." Ma extra-envelops Pickle now, hugging her own warmth into the dog. Pickle doesn't seem to mind one little bit. And if Pickle did mind, I am sure I have no idea what that would look like. "Leave it to you, Alexander," she says. "After seventeen years, you do finally wangle a pet into our midst, and it turns out to be a complete fixer-upper."

"Well, I will fix her up," he says defiantly.

"*We* will fix her up," Ma says.

HELPLESS

But they were both wrong. Pickle is dead on the kitchen floor the next morning when we get up. Ma actually wells up, for the second time in a week, which is about all the wellings I have ever seen from her. She is the one who scoops up the little body, cradling her exactly the same way she did with the live Pickle only the day before. Probably I should have picked it up, since I was the first one out there and found her. But I couldn't do it. Even in life that dog gave me a peculiar form of the creeps, and death had done nothing to improve her "presence."

Ma, holding Pickle, stroking her, speaking low and reassuring words to her, is connecting to this strange little dead thing in a way that catches me by surprise.

But it is nothing compared with the reaction Alexander has

when he comes out for his Quaker instant oatmeal and finds that his brand-new dog is brand-new gone.

You would swear that this was a very close friend or relative who had died. You would swear, at the very least, that the dog that died was a trusted and beloved member of the household for fifteen years, rather than hours.

And he's not being dramatic, which he surely can be. This is for real. Alexander is grieving.

"It was not your fault," Ma says as Alexander just about pries Pickle out of her hands. "There was nothing you could have done in that short space of time. We don't even know how old Pickle was. She could have just passed away of old age, for all we know."

"She wasn't old," he says grimly. He holds her, squeezes her, brings his soul windows right up in front of hers. "I'm sorry, sweetheart," he says to Pickle. "Nobody ever did you any good, did they? You were always with the wrong people at the wrong time. I don't suppose you'd have even died if I'd just left you where you were."

"No," Ma says, "that was a wonderful thing you did, Alexander."

"Yeah," I add. "Think of it like one of those Make-A-Wish things, or a last big day out like they do for terminal human patients. You got the sad little thing out of the cage for the last day of her life, man. Just think about that."

He won't, of course. Or, rather, he will try, and fail, to see the upside there. His own nature will defeat him again and he will flog himself for whatever wrong thing he imagines he's done, or the right thing he failed to do. But just between me and that little husk of dead dog, I know for certain she is in a better place than she was in yesterday when she got here. Hell, she even looks more lively.

"You have to be able to do something. You have to be able to help. How can we be so helpless?"

I don't really have an answer for him, partly because there is no answer for him. I see the spiral, and he will continue downward with this until he is ready to come back up, and not before.

"I have to go to work," I say. Which is sort of an answer, after all. "And so do you," I add.

He is walking out the door with his familiar bowed head as I say it. He always did this when we were kids, though we never had true pets. Squirrels, frogs, salamanders, birds, his findings were the unknown soldiers of the roadkill world. Unknown soldiers in unmarked graves. He managed to find them all space on the periphery of the scrubby patch that passes for a backyard here. More than once we turned up old bones while interring new ones. It's not a lot of yard, but this is not a lot of dog, and she will be given a good and proper send-off before my brother goes to sell anybody any cleaning products this morning.

When I am ready and headed out the door, just after Ma has already gone, I realize he has not reappeared.

"Aren't you worried about being late?" I say when I find him sitting on the ground, in front of an improbably small grave of freshly turned earth.

"I have flexibility. As long as I get a certain amount of crappy work accomplished over the course of the crappy day and the crappy week, and I make my crappy numbers, my crappy supervisor doesn't care how or when it gets done."

"That good, huh?"

"I may be dressing it up a bit."

"Still," I say, patting his back and heading off, "it's a job."

"Still," he sighs, "it is."

I walk along the side of the house, toward the front, and when I get there, the suit slime shark is there again.

"She is not at home," I say to him without stopping.

"I'm going to catch her eventually," the Shark says.

The words give me an instant chill.

I'm going to catch her.

This, this man here. This flesh-eating bacteria was the kind of person I had in mind when I told Alexander that I do, in fact, fantasize about killing. Because I do, and I have. There is violence that just explains itself so straight and simple in your head that you know on a deep level that God or whoever would have to forgive you for it. If I for one second thought I could make my mother's existence a little less tortured, and probably help out a whole lot of his other victims at the same time, and if I thought I could pull it off, I would do this man harm. And I would apologize to nobody.

I turn and walk back to him. "That's my mother you are talking about, filth."

"I'm sorry to hurt your feelings and all, but that's the way it goes. This is my job, and I am going to catch her. I got no sympathy for the likes of you people. You don't like me? Well, boo-hoo. Stop spending money you don't have."

"What is he saying?" It's Alexander, and he has marched right up from the other side. "Catch her? Is he talking about Ma?"

"He is," I say, and now we have the Shark basically sandwiched between us. He is big, looking down at me. He shifts and angles, trying not to have Xan behind him, but Xan shifts and angles to keep him off balance. He does such an effective job, the guy never even gets a proper look at him.

My twelve-year-old self has this vision right now of Xan crouching down behind the guy and me pushing him over. Fun, but not really a long-term solution.

My eighteen-year-old self has another vision, involving the aluminum baseball bat that's under my bed and the guy's brains visible on the sidewalk.

"Don't get cute, boys, or it'll cost you. I am the one legally in the right here."

This little three-way dance to nowhere goes on for several moments, and while it is awkward and testy, it never quite gets the feel of something that's going to truly kick off. Alexander, though, seems more and more intent on not letting the guy get his sights on him, and when the guy does catch up, he gives a quizzical look, like Alexander's face means something.

"I told you she is not here," I say, "so go spook somebody else. I am sure you have plenty of that to do."

He stops flat, doesn't bother anymore with the jockeying. "You know, I do," he says. The thing is, he says it flatly, without malice, without anger or triumph or defeat or pity or anything at all. It shakes me up, frankly, the ghost-hollowness of his voice as he stares right into me. "I have plenty to do. There is a lot of this around, lucky for me."

And like a ghost, a big bulky substance of a sour-smelling spirit, he is, just like that, no longer trapped between my brother and me but street-side and striding off. I stare after him for a few, then turn the other way to find that Alexander has drifted off just as quickly. I catch sight of him as he curves around to the top landing.

"See ya," I call to him.

"See ya," he calls without looking down.

Babette can do the impossible, which I already knew, but now it reaches impressive new heights.

"I cannot believe you got a genuine girl to like my sad-sack brother."

"I appreciate your view of my powers, Robert, but I did no such thing. I simply asked Carly what she thought of him. When she said she thought he was a nice guy, deep and serious—"

"She *likes* serious. . . . Oh, this is too perfect."

"So I just facilitated. No trick, really."

"Thanks anyway, but modesty aside, I'm sticking with my Babette's Powers theory."

We are sitting in a cozy booth under low reddish light in a restaurant called Olde City Walls. It is a partly Middle Eastern and completely vegetarian restaurant that I did not select. The idea of the place is to jazz it up enough and price it down enough to make distant culture and eggplant-based dishes as palatable and cheap for a young clientele as a slice of pizza is. Not a bad concept, the cheap part in particular.

The main reason we are here, though, is that Carly turns out to be a dedicated vegetarian. So dedicated that she has been known to weep when a former animal arrives even on someone else's plate.

"Shouldn't they be here by now?" Babette asks, snagging the last of the four green olives from the complimentary bowl.

"All shoulds are off when it comes to the amazing Mr. A. If he gets her here at all, we are already into the bonus."

The music is kind of Greekish with that instrument that drives me nuts—bouzouki? zither?—but they somehow make it rock at the same time. It is just loud enough for you to be able to talk without ever forgetting it's there.

"Bonus!" I say as I spy the happy couple coming through the door.

Alexander looks boyishly happy at guiding his date through the place. A helpless slap of a smile keeps jumping up onto his face, and he is careful to do all the little gent things like holding the door, putting a light hand on her back as he falls in behind her. He is no ladies' man by anybody's reckoning, and is light on experience, but he appears to have been studying up for this.

He slides into the booth side with me, leaving the ladies across from us in the chairs.

"Hiya, Carly," I say, giving her a wave.

She looks at me almost sheepishly, even physically withdrawing ever so slightly.

"Oh, it wasn't that bad," I say, laughing.

It wasn't. It wasn't a horrible breakup between us, more of a fizzle. We just saw things very differently back then. Increasingly differently. Like, toward the end I found a new, big fat difference pretty much daily. Mostly it came down to a clash of her growing spirituality versus my constant whining for sexual stuff. She maintained that her yearning was more profound than mine. I maintained that hers was not provable and mine was.

"Have you found Jesus yet, Robert?" Carly asks, not as unfriendly as it sounds.

"I didn't even know he was lost, the rascal."

My right shin, the one that is centrally planted under the table, receives a sharp kick. I look around at my companions. There is no shortage of suspects.

Carly is not one of them, however. She smiles the generous smile of a person with a good sense of humor in spite of her approach to matters of every kind of flesh.

"So, you guys," says my date, "tell us a little bit about the class. And about you two getting together."

Alexander does such a full-body recoil of shyness, it catches my eye and I turn right toward him. I give him the imp grin. He reaches right over and pushes my face away and back in the direction of the others.

"The class," Carly says. "Well, it's not like any other class I've ever taken, that's for sure. The instructor, Mr. Fogerty, is like some complete raised-from-the-dead hippie from the 1960s who was at every major protest or demonstration or whatnot since the Vietnam War. He looks like a skinny Sasquatch with all his hair, and wears demonstrator clothes all the time, baggies and sandals with wool fuzzy socks—just in case there is a spontaneous march or something he might miss out on—but he talks really softly like a bishop."

"He's amazing, Mr. Fogerty," Xan says. "He's into all the good causes. He has so much passion."

"How come you never told me any of this?" I ask him.

"You never asked."

"What if I asked?"

"Leave me alone."

"It's true, though," Carly continues. "Mr. Fogerty is a

champion of basically every cause that comes up. Even if one cause seems to conflict with an earlier cause, like conserving dying fish stocks and saving the local fish industry, he seems to support them both."

The cause I support right now is ending hunger at this particular table. The waiter has arrived to support me in this. Before I can open my mouth, Alexander cuts in with an inspired idea.

"Since Carly knows more about all this than we do, why don't we let her order for everybody?"

In response to this mad and dangerous idea, I open my mouth again to speak. Again I am trumped.

"Excellent idea," Babette says.

Carly does indeed seem quite the expert as she rifles through a selection of share-friendly beast-friendly platters as I try to keep up on the menu. Like with a film that has subtitles, I attempt to follow along with what she's ordering, more interested in prices than flavors.

"How much money you got on you?" I whisper to my brother before she is even finished.

"See," he says, "here's the thing . . ."

Has anything good ever followed an opening line of "Here's the thing"?

"Dammit, Alexander," I whisper, as whispering becomes difficult.

"I'm sorry, but I haven't been paid yet. I meant to talk to you about it, but I was so nervous and . . . Come on, that is what big brothers are for, aren't they?"

"No," I say.

By the time this little sub-conversation ends, the food ordering has been sorted. We turn back to the girls to find them grinning our way and whispering themselves. Whispering more effectively than I was, apparently.

"Don't worry," Babette eventually mouths to me. Then she presses down reassuringly on my foot with hers.

"It has started attracting all kinds, to be honest," Carly says, returning to the class subject. "It is good, lots of energy, lots of free expression . . . but it's getting kind of uncomfortable, cramped because of the professor's come-one, come-all policy. And there are certainly some fringies among us, that's for sure."

Reaching for high comedy, I start gesturing toward my fringe-dwelling sibling with my thumb. Reaching for higher comedy, he grabs my thumb and bends it painfully backward.

"Ahh," I shout, quietly, while everyone enjoys the show.

Next thing I know, Alexander is on his feet.

"Harry," he calls, and the two meet in the middle of the restaurant, embracing like lifelong lost pals. Harry has arrived with a handful of his own associates, but none with the obvious might and star power of himself. I am guessing that Harry is used to being in leadership-type roles. But damn, that's a fine Fu Manchu. That mustache could be a leader of men all on its own. I have to attempt one.

"Damn, that is one handsome man," Babette says, quite unnecessarily.

I turn to see her, leering and giggling simultaneously. The effect is surprisingly hot.

I turn to Carly, and find something altogether different. As Harry and Alexander conduct their impromptu close meeting a few feet away, Carly stares in something less than approval. I'm not even sure what you would call her expression, but the situation has caused her eyes to produce two completely separate effects. One eye narrowed like for suspicion or contempt, the other wide in something like fear.

"He is such a great guy," Alexander says, taking his seat as Harry and company move to a separate room.

Carly's silent lack of agreement resounds. Except with Alexander, who appears not to get it.

The conversation goes a little bit flat between now and when the food arrives, but as the waiter sets the variety of vegi tapas around the table, it loosens up again.

"This smells divine," Babette says. "That is what I love about vegetarian food, the combination of spices, of scents and textures that you don't get from, like, chicken in a basket."

Now she's done it. I am actually salivating, thinking about chicken in a basket.

"I think I am going to start eating vegetarian from now on," Xan says, completing a sampler plate for himself and digging in.

I don't even get worked up here because I am certain this is just a ploy to gain favor with Carly. It seems to have an effect, though, as her hard look softens into a gentle smile at him.

"Jeez, that was easy," I say to her.

The kick again, and my shin is stinging. Again, could have been anyone.

"It's true, though," Babette says, wiping her mouth of some falafel and yogurt mint dip. "When you think about it, it gets harder and harder to eat animal products."

Really? I'm thinking about it, and it's having the opposite effect. My shin and I keep that thought to ourselves.

"Oh, you could not be more right," Carly says, putting her hand on Babette's for extra connection. "The way they are treated, even the best feed animals, no matter what the producers say, no matter if they are organic or whatever, it's horrible. Like, 'Here you go, cow buddy. Here's some nice golden corn and grass for lunch. Oh, by the way, bam, here's a bolt shot in your temple.'"

How is it possible that this conversation is making me hungrier? The food here is good. It is tasty and filling and exotic, and . . . it's not meat.

Babette keeps eating and nodding and I am beginning to worry for our future meals. But worse still is Alexander's reaction. He has stopped eating. I look over, and he is weirding out something awful. He's doing the nose-twitch, chin-pucker, lip-withdraw face so familiar to me from all those slights, all those perceived hurts over all those years. When he makes this face, it is no different—not one tic different—from the same kid's face it was five and seven and eleven years ago.

"And that's just the farm animals," he says, his voice fat with sad. "Tell them some of the other stuff."

Carly is staring at my brother with real fondness, I see. I am all over everywhere on this one now. One of my greatest desires at this point in life is for someone, perhaps a female someone, to come along and see the sweetness, the deep-seated lovability, beyond the curtain of strange enveloping my brother, and then want to contribute to making him happy. Appearances are that this is the baby-steps stage of exactly that phenomenon.

But my doubting self cannot help but get a peek in too. Not that I doubt the lovely Carly, who I know from the past, and re-know from the now, is about as genuine and sincere as flawed humanity can manage. But I wonder about the mix, of Alexander and anyone. He has a tendency to become infatuated, led, overly influenced. It has occurred to me at times that Alexander's opinions can appear to be suspiciously similar to those of the last person he's spoken to. It is not because he is stupid or weak-minded. It is not.

It is because he cares so much, and because he wants, so much, to belong. He wants what you want. Because he wants to be with you.

So his companions' beliefs matter much in the big picture. And Carly's beliefs run serious.

Among the "fringies," it becomes obvious that her own niches are animal rights and the Lord Jesus Christ.

But, for this instant, she has another interest that at least temporarily shades them both.

She leans a bit over the table toward my brother, leaving his request for an animal rights discourse hanging momentarily.

"Would you take your glasses off for a minute?" she says.

It feels like a hush falls over the whole room. This is an awkward turn of events, as things were progressing so nicely, but I know Xan is not ready to be opening his soul windows to just—

"So lovely," Carly says.

And I turn to see him, sitting rigidly upright, fidgeting with the glasses in his hands but giving her full access.

"Have you considered getting contacts, or at least clear lenses? You're not light sensitive, are you? Just seems a shame to hide those big soft eyes from the rest of the world."

And just like that, the big soft eyes retreat behind their color-coordinated defense.

"Sensitive is right," I say helpfully.

But the progress is made, and Carly soldiers bravely on to tell us what happens right here in our own backyard, to the blinded and shocked and stung test bunnies at the university, to the driven-demented beakless chickens living cozy by the thousands in their cages at the state's third-largest-employer farm, and of course, those unfortunate stunned-and-skinned-but-not-always-necessarily-in-that-order minks at the fur factory just up the road.

Dinner chat unlike any other, you'd have to say.

And everybody's response is different. Babette calmly puts down her silverware at the mention of the first bald university monkey and does not resume eating. I keep eating, being only too aware that there is nothing tortured and fleshy on these plates, while at the same time I cannot take my eyes and ears off the story or the teller. It is grimly riveting stuff, and I am rapidly educated well beyond what I thought I knew.

Alexander becomes catatonic. And I believe he has already heard most of it before.

Carly stops talking, and takes in the scene around her. As it will happen with people who are passionate and/or nuts about their pet topics, she somewhere lost the connection between the words and the events and reactions around her.

"Sorry about that," she says, putting her head in her hands and staring down at her plate. She does then go on to pick at her food.

"Not at all, hon," Babette says, reaching over and giving her a hug. "You just care a lot about this, and that's wonderful."

Alexander emerges from his trance.

"We have to do something," he says grimly. "You cannot just go on and on, not doing anything about anything. You can't."

"Social responsibility, right?" Babette says, raising her water glass.

I shake my head discreetly at her, trying to stem the tide of my brother's excitability, but the tide is in anyway.

"Social responsibility," the others all add, clinking glasses, though I come in a bit late and spoil the unity effect somewhat.

Despite its kinks, the evening has to be considered a real success, capped off by Alexander heading off to walk Carly home, while Babette and I walk the other way toward her place.

"Did you see them holding hands just there?" Babette says. As we ourselves walk, I attempt one of those big heavy round-the-neck hugs that look all affectionate but make getting down the sidewalk quite a chore. Just as affectionately she removes my arm and places it around her waist. This works nicely.

"I did see that," I say. "I'm still in shock. I don't even remember him holding my mother's hand. I'll have to check with her."

"I wouldn't," she says.

"Did you like your food?" I ask.

"I did, as much of it as I could eat."

"Yeah, me too. I'll tell you, we see any roadkill on the way home, I'm eating it."

"Barf."

We are approaching Babette's place, and I am winding up to start suggesting the many ways I would like to thank her for picking up approximately 60 percent of the check, when she cuts me off at the pass.

"Thank you for a lovely evening," she says, sticking out her hand for me to shake.

I stare at this strange and unsettling thing, as if she is offering me a peeled mink on a stick.

"Explain?" I say.

"Well, I found your old girlfriend very inspiring tonight. So I thought I'd give the whole no-meat, no-nookie thing a go. The Lord is my burger and my satisfaction."

I continue to stare at the hand, trying to work out what has happened to my universe.

"This is because I have no money, isn't it?"

I have never enjoyed being slapped in the face more.

"Yeow," I say, rubbing my cheek, though it was hardly a tap. We are both laughing.

"That'll teach you to go dutch with me, ya cheap SOB."

"I have to work in the morning anyway," I say, walking backward down the sidewalk as she stands on the bottom step to her house.

"No good night kiss for me?" she says, arms open.

"Actually, I'm kind of still savoring the slap," I tell her.

She gives me a nod of some satisfaction and blows me a kiss before heading up and in.

If my brother can manage half the slap I got, this will have been a wildly successful evening.

NIGHT AND DAY

My alarm goes off at quarter to six, like it does every workday. I slap it on top of its sleep-shattering head, like I do every workday, getting another ten minutes of snooze-button reprieve. I always use the full ten.

In two minutes my eyes pop open like they are spring-loaded and I sit right up in bed.

He's not home.

Alexander never came home.

My first response, which I am sure I share with the spirit of the entire universe, is one of unbridled delight.

My second response, personal to myself alone, is, "So, what was wrong with me?" How on earth does—of all people, come on now—Alexander break the Carly code so quickly after I was so comprehensively unsuccessful at it?

I won't have to wait long to find out, because as soon as I formulate the question, he appears in the room.

"You dog," I say with undisguised admiration and, even more generous, envy. "How the hell did you manage it?"

"What?" he says wearily, lying right down on his bed with his clothes on.

I swing my legs over and plant my bare feet firmly on the floor between us.

"You know what. Carly, what. How did you so easily go where no man has gone before?"

"Be quiet, Robert, okay? You don't even know what you're talking about."

"Yes, I do." I get to my feet and lean over him. "I can smell you. Your whole body chemistry has changed already."

He gives me a good mighty shove that topples me backward onto my bed again.

"You know nothing about me, or my body chemistry, so just stop right there."

"Jeez, kid, I live in the same room with you. I know all. I know more about you than you do."

"Wrong," he says, closing his eyes.

"Really? Don't you think I know you've spanked more monkey than any mother monkey ever—"

"That's it. I'm leaving again." He pops right up, and sweeps out of the room.

I hear him start the shower. I start getting myself dressed. Then he sweeps back in again while the shower is running, and gathers some new clothes. I brush past him, inhaling his musk once more.

Stronger than I realized, actually.

"Jeez. Is that what that scent is, Xan? It's kinda . . . pungent."

His glasses are off, back in the bathroom. He wheels on me and the eyes are really wide, really wild, really meaning it.

"Shut up, Robert. Do you get me? Shut yourself up, now."

And for one of the rare moments of my life, I take that advice.

By the time I come out dressed for work, he has left the shower, and the house again. Ma emerges from her room and joins me for coffee.

"Did I hear your brother leave already?" she asks.

"I think you did, yeah."

"To work?"

"I guess so. I guess he's extra motivated because he still doesn't have any money."

Ma's face mostly disappears inside her oversize coffee mug. The echo of her voice is also oversize in there when she makes her sound, "Hnn."

I sip my coffee. Take a bite of toast. I offer her a bite, though I know she won't touch food until coffee number two is under way.

"Bite?" I ask.

"No, but thank you."

"It's got marmalade."

More definitive. "No. But. Thank you."

I bite. I sip. She sips. She sips.

"About that," I say gingerly. "Money, and not-money . . ."

"It's fine, Robert," she says, tripping off to the Mr. Coffee again. "We are all working now, things are steady, we are getting someplace. It's all good."

I nod. "I could probably give you more. And Alexander—"

"Thank you," she says. "Maybe. We'll see how it goes. But it'll be all right. Don't lose sleep over it."

She is settled now at her head-of-table spot, to my left, looking out toward the front window again. Settled with that second big cup.

"I'll make you some toast now," I say.

She shakes her head. "Not just yet, Robert, thanks."

So I stare at her. Very consciously, though I know she doesn't like that. I don't care. Her eyes are dark, her cheeks deflated from their usual healthy plump.

"How much money, Ma?" I ask quietly, like who are we hiding from?

She waves me off.

I won't be waved off.

"It's large," I say.

"For us? Large."

"How, Ma?"

"How." She bites the word off, angry—not at me. At the word, maybe. "How? Look at the news, Son. Look at the world. Look out the window. Look at this building. Look at *us*. When things go bad, they go bad *here*. You work at a job, and you're glad to have it. Then times go tough and people stop spending and they stop tipping you, and your bills don't go down just because some slick thinks that your tip, your necessity, is suddenly his option, his maybe-not. Then you fall behind, and then a little more. Then you try to catch up, then you try harder, then you try something else, then you try, in the end, something stupid. You go for a lifeline that is really not, and it only makes things really worse, really quickly, and you realize you have done something really, really stupid."

Helpless. Furious and helpless is all I can manage as I look at my mighty mother crumbling in the seat in front of me, in the same chair where she has provided all the thousands of meals over all those years and never missed one, and saw to it that the three of us made a point of sitting right here and eating it all together.

I can only think of one thing to do.

"I am making you some damn toast right now," I say, jumping up so crazy from my chair that it flips over backward.

Her eyes, sad gray slashes a second ago, go round and buggy at me now.

And she bursts into a blurt of coffee-scented laughter that caffeinates the whole house.

"Did you just get tough with me, over toast?" she asks, incredulous.

"Yes, I did," I snap, still displacing anger inappropriately all over the joint.

"Well, then," she says. "I guess I'd better have some damn toast, then!"

"Well, dammit, all right, then," I say to her.

"Fine, dammit. You had better go get my damn toast, then, hadn't you?"

I go directly to the toaster as Ma giggles into her mug. I'm feeling a little better than I did when I watched her beautiful face aging like stop-motion in front of my eyes. It's not much, dammit, but it's something.

Things calm down over toast. Most things are calmable with toast, I think, especially with the right marmalade.

"This is good," Ma says.

"Thick shred," I say proudly as if I made it myself. "Lemon *and* lime. Nick at the garage gave it to me. Customer gave him this food basket with all kinds of stuff in it. Nick doesn't like marmalade, the madman."

She nods, eats. "Things will get better, Robert. Things are getting better. If we just keep up. If we just don't fall too far behind."

I nod, happy enough that she's opening up this much. "We will do better. We'll all do better. We'll get there."

We are both believing, both nodding, when the ringing of the phone cuts like a screaming missile through the house. Ma startles, drops her toast. Then she drops her eyes, then her shoulders, her chin.

"Already?" she says wearily. "So early?"

I jump up to answer it.

"Go to work, Robert," she insists as the phone rings viciously again, then again. "Don't answer that. Go to work. That's the best you can do, is go to work."

It was so nice there, for a minute. It was so better.

I am certain I could kill that man if he turned up on our doorstep now.

It is a short workday for me, which is really not what we need at this point. I was on the verge of asking Nick for more hours, but there are no more hours. He doesn't have the need, or the extravagant profit margin, to be offering me any more. And I, with school commitments, don't really have any more to give him.

Which is why this is a short day. I have to knock off halfway through and get home to clean up for one of the truly great assignments of my college program. I have to get over to the middle school and run my own phys ed class. It's the kind of placement that is routine in the sports coaching and development degree program, but it is not routine to me. I am excited, scared, unsure, thrilled, ready, lost.

So, I am back home by noon, in the house and half stripped already by the time I get to the bedroom.

"I thought you were at work," I say to the unexpected brother lying on his bed.

I have surprised him more than he did me, and he nervously tucks away the book he was reading. I caught enough of a glimpse to know it wasn't *that* kind of amusement, but not enough to get what the problem was.

"And I thought *you* were at work," he says, eyeballing me as I sweep past.

"I am at work," I say, gathering up my nicest-looking dark blue tracksuit—the gym teacher's business suit—that I had laid out the night before. I am about to go from one physical job to another, but because their two scents are very different and it's not cool to drag one to the other, I have to take a short shower.

"So, you're a work-at-home grease monkey now," he says. "That must be a trick."

I stop at the doorway, my clothes over my arm. "Garage was this morning. This afternoon I have a placement, for the college.

Teaching gym at the middle school. And I'm pretty anxious, so don't be in my way."

I leave him there on his bed to go back to reading whatever weirdness I couldn't know about.

I scrub myself silly in the shower, suddenly consumed with the notion of making an impression. Who am I supposed to impress? Kids? Teachers? Administrators? Will my performance get me a job one day? A good grade this semester? I cast around, but cannot come up with a sure result to what a great day today does for my life. In fact, as well as I know this particular middle school, I will be surprised if anyone even realizes I was there at the end of it all.

And still, I am consumed.

I want something better. I want something more. I want, I want, I want, and I am very aware that to get, to get, to get, a guy is going to have to go through a lot of assessment. A lot of judging by people who already are there, who have already got.

I scrub like a maniac, even though I already scrubbed at the garage. I am not sure how much thick dirty motor oil still clings to me, how much is still visible or smellable, but it doesn't matter because I have to just stop. I stop, but only because I run out of time.

"The Dean?" Alexander says when I come back into the room looking like the shiniest, most professional phys ed instructor anybody ever had. Perhaps inspired by me, he has changed into similar, though not as sharp, track attire. He's stretching for a run. "Are you working at the Dean?"

"The one and only Dean Middle School, yes," I say.

"Wow," he says. He pauses while I check myself in the mirror, then pipes out when I try to get out the door. "Any chance I could come?"

It's a silly idea.

It's an inspired idea.

"Technically, probably not," I say. "They tend to be kind of strict about nonessential personnel tagging along for laughs."

"I'm not for laughs," he says in pitch-perfect Alexander seriousness.

"No, that's for sure," I say. "Maybe you could just kind of escort me there, be around for moral support, and stay out of the way. You could just be a graduate of the old Dean back for a visit, right? I don't think anybody could be too bothered by that."

"And," he adds flatly, "it's the Dean. I don't think they could get too bothered by *anything*."

He's got a point there. And I am really glad to have his company.

"Ramshackle" is probably as good a term as any to describe the Dean of our day. Physically the place could have used a lot more attention than it got. Heavy rains always produced a pattern of buckets sprouting like mushrooms from hallway floors all over to catch the drops, and the huge tall windows in most classes would be weeping and as wet on the inside as on the outside. There was almost never any evidence of repair work going on, the explanation invariably that the school committee report had the school earmarked for a total teardown/rebuild that was going to make us the envy of the system. The school committee must have recycled that report every year, because nothing ever got done, and the hulking yellow brick structure that is appearing now as Xan and I crest the small Creighton Street hill has obviously had nothing applied to it but years.

"You been back here at all since?" I ask Alexander, as much to make small talk as anything. Honestly, you would think I was going for an interview at the White House, I am filled with such anticipation.

"What reason would I have for that?" he says, staring at the old monstrosity.

"Tell me again why you are not at work?"

"Can't tell you again because I didn't tell you once."

"Tell me why you are not at work?"

"Don't you have enough on your plate right now?"

"Ah, cripes, Xan . . ."

"Just get through this first, huh?"

He is quite right. As the building comes closer, the nerves fritz louder, until we are through the big chain-link gates, and walking across the frost-heaved potholed asphalt playground.

Which, surprisingly, helps. It's a funny phenomenon, that from the approach—from the outside of the gate, even—the school had its connection for me, its memories and suggestions. But outside the gate was nothing at all, a different experience entirely, compared to the moment my feet actually hit the playground, this decrepit has-been of a playing surface with its painted lines for basketball and hopscotch and street hockey.

"Wow," I say to my brother as I hesitate, looking up at the gables, down at the cracks and white lines, over at the netless basketball hoops. "Do you feel it, Alexander?"

"I do," he says, looking up, down, over. "This might be the suckiest place on Earth."

With a delivery as flat as his, Alexander could be as likely joking as not. But with my privilege of all that background information, I know he's not.

It can't help me from laughing out loud, though.

"Oh, come on, man," I say, loosening up, punching his shoulder. "Surely you can't remember it all that bad."

He punches me back, an entirely different thing. It stings.

"Surely I can," he says.

I laugh out loud again, and I am forced at the same time to recognize that this was, is, part of Alexander's problem. I was always having fun even if, sometimes especially if, he was not. All I can recall of this scruffy playground—and that is probably three quarters of my entire school recollection—is fun and success. Hockey goals and perfect hip checks and the best kind of fights. Three-on-three basketball games with scores that seemed to go into the millions. Throwball, which was nothing more than baseball played with a tennis ball, and you threw the ball into play instead of pitching and hitting it, and you got the other guy out by whipping the ball at him. I still have a mark above my left knee that I am certain came from Ramon Alfonso drilling me perfectly from forty feet away. That's how you knew you were popular, taking one on the leg—if the likes of Ramon didn't like you, you wound up blinded in one eye, or unable to have children. Soccer was always my game, my calling card, but they were all my games, really. I wasn't extraordinary. There was this whole tier of guys, specialists at something, good at everything. I was one, and life was good.

Alexander was something other.

"I must have taken two hundred tennis balls straight in the forehead during the time I was here," Xan says.

I don't know if he is creating this awkward situation on purpose or not, but there is nothing I can do about it. I have my hands on my knees, wheezing, I am laughing so hard.

"I know," I say, "and, what, were, like, eighty of them from me?"

"Conservative estimate," he says, with dignity I could only dream of.

Checking my watch, I realize my excitement has us here well early. Old times' sake hasn't got to make way just yet.

"Let's do a walk-around," I say.

Alexander shrugs a yes.

It's a big building—huge building, really, for what it is. Kids, little kids, spend their middle school years here, learning much or not much of anything, acting up and playing out and whatnot. My brother and I walk the perimeter of the building, and I realize like I never did before that this place is its own thing, its own neighborhood, its own world.

"God," I say, turning a corner, looking up, looking around.

"God," Alexander says, though he sounds less shocked than me.

It might as well be the Pentagon. One corner turns onto another one, and the grounds seem to go on forever. A remnant of the earliest days, a hundred and fifty or so years ago when the place was built, there is a stout beech tree bursting right up out of the black asphalt. Alexander and I, without talking about it, go straight to the tree, lean on opposite sides without looking at each other.

"The best of times," I say, theatrically.

"The worst of times," he says, no joke.

"Come on, pal," I say. "You are being dramatic. Stop making it sound worse than it was."

I am looking up at the great bank of windows that flood light into the classrooms and allow the world to look in on them. If the world cares to look.

"Do you even know how it was?" he says.

"Of course I do," I say. "It was great. And I was thinking it must have been even greater for you, being the younger brother of the king."

It would be very difficult to describe my brother's expression here as he walks around to stare at me on my side of the tree. He's a little bit of both perplexed and angry.

"You honestly still believe that, don't you?"

I shrug. "Is that a trick question? Yes, I believe it. I mean, sure, I could be a pain, but there were also benefits to having me, I assume."

His scowl deepens, ridges carving up his forehead like on a Klingon. "You know, you never once put me on a team of yours? And you were always a captain, so it was always up to you."

"That can't be true. I remember at least one time. It was late, probably June, really hot out. We were playing throwball."

"You didn't pick me. You just ran out of other guys to pick. Then, halfway through the game, you traded me. Remember that?"

"Oh, God," I say, trying to stifle what is surely another poorly timed laugh. "I traded you for half a bottle of Gatorade."

"Ah, sweet of you to remember."

"Well, yeah. Turned out the Gatorade was mostly backwash anyway. If it makes you feel better, I think I barely broke even on that trade."

He just turns and walks. I trot to catch up.

"You shouldn't take stuff like that so seriously, Alexander. You were always taking stuff so seriously."

He is not fuming here. He is not whining or snapping at me or getting in any way overly emotional. But calmly and flatly his words are laying me out.

"You never picked me, Robert. And I wasn't even that bad."

"No, you were pretty good," I admit. And as his argument gets stronger, mine falters badly. "I just . . . It was a long time ago. And things like that, they don't mean anything."

"I had a hard time."

"Yeah, but lots of guys—"

"You never had my back. Never. And that mattered. A lot."

"That is not true," I say as we turn the last corner back to the front of the building. "I may have given you a hard time and all, but when the chips were down, I was always there for you."

He stops short and faces me. He points to a spot a few feet back, to that corner. "Right there, Brother. The chips were down, right there. That is where Bruce Brown kicked the daylights out of me. Had me crying like a baby in front of half the school and everything. And were you *there* for me? No, you were *there*." He points over to the basketball hoop.

"I don't remember this, Alexander," I say.

"I imagine you don't. Everybody else was either shouting up the fight or running toward it, but you couldn't leave your game. But I am sure it was a close game. . . ."

I don't remember this. But I don't doubt it either.

"I'm sorry," I say. "Bruce Brown was . . ."

"A mother," he says with a very complicated small laugh. He

shakes his head with the memory. "And when I went after him, with the janitor's big thick broom handle . . ."

Oh. Oh, cripes, I do remember this.

"They gave you a week's suspension," I say.

"That was the point when everyone started acting different toward me, thinking I wasn't right. I still had another whole year to do in this place, and everybody thought there was something mentally disarranged about me. I wasn't homicidal. I was just . . . scared.

"It was lonely. That next year was. Really lonely."

Abruptly Alexander decides that is the end of his story. He spins and walks toward the front of the school. Again, I catch up with him.

"I should have been there, Xan. I always should have been there. Things should have been different."

We are standing side by side in front of the big imposing doors of the Dean Middle School.

"I have forgiven you," he says with a sly smile that indicates he probably knows what a cut that is.

"Thanks," I say.

As we push through the great green wooden doors into the gray marble foyer of the school, we must look like a pair of gym teacher brothers with our outfits. But the look does the trick, because a small man with a big clipboard comes right up to us.

"Robert, is it?" the man says, extending a hand.

"Yes, sir," I say, some of the nerves coming back with the sudden officialness of it all. "You must be Mr. Genarro?"

"I am. We don't have a lot of time. The kids are in the gym

already. You've got one of our lower-rung eighth-grade classes. I think you'll find them . . . spirited."

"Spirited is good."

"Ya think? Let me know what you think after fifty-five minutes of spirit."

The foyer and adjoining corridors are largely empty, as it is the start of the period. A couple of stragglers scatter as Mr. Genarro leads me toward the gym. He struts like a bantam rooster.

"Kind of ghostly," I say, not recalling it ever like this.

"Student numbers are actually very low, compared to what the school was built for. Been down for years now."

Still looking around, and with Alexander coming along behind me, we nearly have a pileup when Genarro stops short. He pivots, having apparently just processed the presence of one too many.

"Who's this?" he asks.

"That's my brother, Alexander."

"Hello," says Alexander.

"Hello," says Genarro, flipping through pages on his clipboard. "I don't have Alexander down here anywhere."

"No, he's just come along with me. See, we both—"

"Can't let that happen, guys. Sorry. No unauthorized—"

The glass partition that is the portal to the main office slides open. It is where the secretary sits, where you cannot get by if you are late, where you must report when things take a turn for the untoward. Behind the secretary are the offices of the top end of the school administration. Right now the bald dome of one of those top ends pokes through the opening.

"Robert?" the man asks tentatively.

"Mr. Wickes?" I ask in return.

Mr. Wickes is possibly the nicest educator I have encountered in my entire life. Sad, efficient, melancholy, understanding, good at his job while looking like he might be thinking about a different one. Once we have established that we are who we think we are, Mr. Wickes comes around and out the door.

"How are you, Robert?" Mr. Wickes says.

"I am really good, thank you, sir."

"You know this fellow, Mr. Wickes?"

"Oh, certainly. Robert here was something of a sporting legend when he was at the school. Still one of our finest products, academically as well. And . . ." Here is where he is classic Mr. Wickes. "Alexander? Alexander, look at you. How are you, son?"

I turn to Xan, and he is, no denying it, all choked up. Mr. Wickes would have been there, on hand, central to sorting out almost all of the many and varied difficulties my brother got into in his years at the Dean. As the assistant head teacher, Mr. Wickes probably spent more time with Xan through that time than anyone else did.

"I'm fine, sir," Xan says softly.

I look at the badge. Mr. Wickes was always the only one on staff who wore it, probably to head off anyone thinking he was a janitor, or a sticky intruder, or some hapless student kept back thirty-five times and trapped within the school walls in a permanent loop of horror. The badge says, like it said when I left here last time, ASSISTANT HEAD TEACHER.

"What brings you here, boys—?" He interrupts himself with his own Wickesiness. "Jeez, it's good to see you kids back—sorry, *men*. To see you *men* back. You look great. Look how you turned out, the two of you."

"Well, Mr. Wickes," Genarro says, "as a matter of fact, we are running a bit late. Robert here is doing a placement as part of his program over at the CC. He's running a gym class for us right now. His brother, I'm afraid, just came with him, and I really don't think I can—"

"I'll take care of it," Mr. Wickes says excitedly, clearly happy to be able to take care of something. He walks with the rest of us toward the gym. "So, Robert, the CC. Marvelous, marvelous. Education?"

"Sports coaching and development, sir."

"Of course," he says excitedly. "This is just terrific. I wish we had a chance to see more of our alumni back here, catching us up on where they are now."

I am thinking what a nice thought that is. I am thinking, it's probably best for Mr. Wickes that most of them just stay away.

"And yourself, Alexander?" Mr. Wickes says with unfeasible hopefulness as we are about to enter the gym. "What are you doing with yourself these days?"

He has his hand on Xan's shoulder as we walk through the gym door. He looks at him so anxiously, it's as if the answer is going to determine whether Mr. Wickes is going to dedicate the rest of his professional days to trying to better the likes of us or cave in to blunt and brutal reality.

Jeez, Mr. Wickes. Jeez, Xan.

"I just started at the CC too, Mr. Wickes."

Attaboy, Alexander.

"Social work," Alexander boldly plows forth.

Mr. Wickes jumps away from Xan, whipping his hand from his shoulder as if untruth were an actual deadly electrical charge running through the boy. He points at Xan.

"I knew it," says a beaming Mr. Wickes. "I absolutely knew it. I was going to guess that. Ah, my boy," he says, patting Alexander with several hard audible thumps on his back. "Perfect, that is. Perfect, perfect. I knew you could do it. I really did know you had it in you."

Mr. Genarro has already introduced me to his bored and irritable-looking gang of thirteen-year-olds, and is bantam-strutting over to the equipment closet. Because we have already eaten up a chunk of prep time, it appears some decisions will not be mine to make. I don't have a leap for joy when I see him dragging across the wide gym floor the gigantic and familiar old gym-hockey bag that will dominate the next small chunk of these kids' educational lives as well as mine. I was kind of thinking soccer, and outside. Almost dwarfed by the bag, the little teacher looks like the Grinch stealing all of Christmas and hauling it to his sleigh.

"Right, son," Genarro says to me, "since you are an esteemed alum, and this bag of sticks is at least twenty-five years old, I will assume you know your way around it."

"Yes, sir," I say.

"And what about this one?" Genarro says to Wickes, indicating my brother.

"Just leave it with me," Mr. Wickes answers. "I'll create some paperwork on it." Then he turns to Xan with a wink. "As an assistant head, it's what I do best."

Genarro exits, satisfied.

"It's a long way from what you do best," Alexander says to Mr. Wickes, shaking his hand as Wickes leaves.

Almost the instant we are left without official Dean staff, we have bedlam. The entire class of thirty or so makes a lunge for the gear bag at once, and I actually jump back a couple of steps to let this happen, the way you do not break up a dog fight, to save your arms. Even with the chaos before me, magnified to a hundred and fifty young maniacs by the old school echo of the place, I am struck by the distinctive sound coming from behind me.

"Heh-heh-heh-heh-heh-heh," etc., etc., comes rolling out of my well-pleased brother. He backs up and sits on the end of the long bench that is up against the wall. "This looks like it's going to be more fun than I thought," he says, folding his arms.

I turn back to the carnage, and it has played out pretty much exactly as Charles Darwin would have said it would. There are twenty sticks for thirty students, and by the time I have swung back around to them, the ten least carnivorous are standing there, stickless, while the others are already digging in the bag for hockey balls.

There are green sticks and blues, so the teams have already selected themselves. I take the unlucky ten, make a chopping motion down the middle of the lineup, and pull half over to the bench Alexander is sitting on. The rest go to the opposite wall and bench. Game on.

It is clear from the opening whistle—which they ignore—that these guys are aware their time is short today, and that they are dealing with a rookie.

It is hockey, all right, but it acts a lot like the magnet-ball style we played at the very lowest levels of soccer. If watched from above, the whole process would resemble a gaggle of metal kids being manipulated by one tiny ball with the world's most powerful magnet inside. No strategy, no positions, no teamwork to speak of. Just get that ball, each and every individual passionately for himself.

Down here on the floor, though, it's a different thing. It's all of the above, but with an impressively high violence level.

"Hey," I scream after my whistle is ignored again, "sticks *down*! Anyone who does not keep the stick below waist level is coming off. . . . Hey!" I scream again, after the whistle, before the next whistle.

The floor is shaking, the sound huge, like a wildebeest stampede, and it turns out walls mean nothing at all to these guys. Boom, I just miss my own collision as a gang of four flies past me and they all hurtle gleefully into the wall. The substitute nearest me is tapping my shoulder like he's knocking on a door, to get me to put him in the game. "In a minute," I tell him. "In a minute." I should embrace the substitutions, since that appears to be my only true job here.

"Hey!" I scream again. "Blue team. If I see that again, all three of you are coming off and you won't go back in."

They have ganged up on a defenseman trying to clear the ball from his own corner. The ball is safely away, while the defenseman is doing a fair impression of a crime scene chalk outline.

"Okay, you're in," I say to my pest. "Get the stick from that guy on the floor."

Next thing, Alexander is beside me and in my ear. "This is intense," he says.

"Tell me about it," I say. "Are these guys on day release, or what?"

"And half of them are as big as us."

"Think I haven't noticed that?"

The next kid along comes up and starts tugging my shirt to get into the game, and I can't help talking with the rhythm and punch of the game. "Inaminute, kid, inaminute."

"Wish there was something I could do to help," Alexander says, backing away and clearly not wishing there was something he could do to help.

"There is," I say, grabbing him by the jacket. "Go over there and coach that team."

"What?" he says. "No way."

"Come on, Xan," I say. "It'll be fun. The class is half over already, and really the only job you have to do is make substitutions so every kid gets a little time."

"No way," he says, yanking himself out of my grip. "This is your problem."

But as he is about to take his safe seat back on the bench, I grab him by something better than his jacket. "Fine," I say, "if you want to sit there and watch the same bunch of kids who probably never get to play anything spend another class not getting to play . . . knowing what that feels like . . ."

I turn my back to him, pretending I have any real impact on the game in front of me. Next thing, I get a good solid smack across the back of my head as Alexander runs across to manage the far bench. It was quite a pop, sending my head right forward, and when I straighten back up again, I swear every single kid in this class is looking my way, whether they are playing the game at full speed or just standing there, and the hall is reverberating with the sound of "Whoooo-hoooo," a sound known to every schoolboy of every era who ever dished out or received an embarrassing cheap shot that the crowd wanted avenged, for their amusement.

How do they do that? They can't hear a whistle louder than a fire engine, but a bap across the back of my head can stop traffic.

Across the way, Xan is leering at me while simultaneously pulling two guys off the floor and replacing them with two of his sadder subs.

They are listening to him. It was the head slap.

The game has become a game. Because Alexander has his guys paying attention, they are getting coordinated. They are passing to each other and manning positions rather than bing-bing-binging around the place. My guys, still unconvinced of my authority, are continuing with the anarchy approach.

In the first three minutes of Xan's regime, his team has scored three times and is thoroughly embarrassing mine. When play comes bashing past me, I reach out and grab one of my more disruptive beasts and replace him with somebody from the bench. The beast is not happy, and I am sure I am ignoring remarks about my mother as I try to coach us to victory.

One thing that has not changed is that the testosterone in this gym is swirling tornado force. They are playing hockey—and clearly have been watching it on TV—but the skills are still taking second priority to the commitment to knocking the stuffing out of one another at every chance.

These boys, I realize, are *angry*. It is not like I remember it. I remember the roughhouse, absolutely. I remember hitting that very wall so hard that I had a hard-boiled egg growing out of the top of my head before I even hit the floor. I even remember the odd fight here and there. But way more than that, I remember the fun. It was fun.

These guys in front of me are so serious, they could be doing this for a job. For very little pay. It's as if they are getting points for pain, or fear, intimidation or anguish, rather than putting the ball in the net.

Am I remembering it wrong? Were we just as bad?

As the clock winds down, they appear to be aware of opportunities getting away from them, because the skill level seems to deteriorate again, in favor of more raw aggression. I look across the way, trying to get my brother's attention with my open palm *What the hell?* gesture. But I can't get him. He is transfixed by what he is seeing. He has become a bystander at a bad accident, watching with his mouth open, wincing with a particularly nasty check, raising his arms as if he is defending his own self when one of my guys suddenly raises his stick and takes a chop at one of his.

"All right, all right," I say, then blow hard on my whistle as I run across the floor. My guy still has his stick raised, while the other one stands defiant, daring him, actually with the old familiar, *Come on, bring it* gesture, with his hands flicking at hip height.

"Sticks *down*," I bellow so loudly that it all but drowns out the monster that is the school-wide bell. That bell could wake the dead, and I always wondered if they'd bought it from an old shipyard or steelworks.

The sticks are down, and I am standing between two kids who, if they decided to, could well leave me in a heap. But the thing that was there at the beginning of this, the apprehension, the over-my-head-ness, is somehow gone. *Gone* as I stand here.

I feel as right and strong in this place as I did when I was their age. But in a different way, from a different angle.

"You two, collect up all the equipment and put it in the bag," I say as the rest of the class wafts away.

"Good," Mr. Genarro says to me as I approach him at the exit. "Well handled. You have to take charge with these guys or you have unfettered madness. I only caught the last few minutes, but how'd you like it? Teach 'em a thing or two, did you?"

I expect Alexander to be the first to laugh, or make a remark, so I turn to him. He's neither laughing nor remarking. He looks dazed, distracted.

I turn back to Mr. G. "No, sir, I'd say it was more like the other way around."

"Ah, well," he says. "That's good too. That's what you're here for as well, right?"

"Right," I say, knowing he could not be righter.

The boys have collected all the equipment in the bag and already vaporized. Mr. G shakes my hand, then Alexander's, and the last we see of him is his little hunched back, bumping away with the Grinch bag across the floor.

"Tell me something, Xan," I say as the two of us make our way down the corridor toward the exit. "Do you recall, when we were here, guys being as angry as this bunch?"

There is enough pause time for me to hear the *pat-pat* of our sneakers on the marble floor.

"I was," he says softly.

My feeling of strength fades, and I do not follow up. I don't care to think about that, to imagine that, to realize the reality of my brother like that and why.

I shut up as we go out the door, and I'm sure that suits Alexander just fine.

We head straight across the asphalt playground, the way we came, until we hear ungodly commotion, baying crowd sounds around the side of the building. Quick-stepping in that direction, we turn the corner of the building, where the noise gets stronger, and we break into a trot. Halfway down the side of the building, the structure takes an inexplicable sharp turn, a sort of alleyway/cave/dead end leading to a door that has been unused except for emergencies for probably forty years. This dark spot looks perverse to me now, a pointless hall of horror, and I don't know why I never noticed before, and I don't know now why anyone would ever build a place like this.

Unless it was to satisfy a bloodthirsty mob and the two brutal warriors at the center of it who need a place to hammer out all the anger there is.

It is, of course, the two guys who wanted at each other at the end of my class, surrounded by mostly that class and whichever other luckies got wind. I bore my way in to find blood already, lots and real and nobody is finished.

Both guys are upright and bleeding, but the guy who was wielding the stick is right now wishing he had not, for I have rarely seen the equal of this in my life. The other guy, slightly smaller, but all Doberman fury and precision, has got him by the collar with one hand and is pounding, pounding, with the other fist. Every punch—must be fifteen shots in the seven seconds I see—lands in one of two *precise* spots. Mouth, mouth, eye, eye, eye, mouth, mouth. . . . The losing guy's lower lip looks like he has spent the afternoon chewing it as hard as he can, and his cheek bone is swelling up in front of his eye. He landed his own last punch before I ever showed up, because his hands now fall right to his sides, and he totters there for more.

Until I burst through and wrap up the puncher in a bear hug.

"All right," I say as he struggles, "it's done." And I'm also thinking, as he jostles me around, *Holy hell, this is one tough bastard here. This as an angry mighty man, no matter how old he is.*

But I've got his arms pinned, and the bloody pulp guy has it just enough together to reach across and snap a punch right off the guy's nose.

So Alexander wraps that guy up, and the next thing I know, my head is screaming, ringing and rocking with pain as I look up to see I've just taken a full-brunt shot just above the temple from a third kid, the one who hated me for taking him out of the game.

"Hey, hey, hey!" I hear then, a familiar voice in an unfamiliar holler.

The crowd bursts like at the start of a race, witnesses scattering to the distances.

"Jeez, people," says Mr. Wickes, a maintenance guy by his side. "Not this stuff. Please, no more of this stuff."

He sees me and my brother in subdue mode. He comes right over to us and physically pries us from the fighters. He tells the boys to stand there with the janitor and pulls us out toward the main yard.

"I thought you guys were going to stop by on your way out?" he says sadly, yet another sampling of obvious pain in this difficult place.

"Sorry, sir," I say. "We were—"

"No mind. We'll see you again, we'll see you again. Listen, this here is not good. This is not the way you are supposed to handle the fightings. This . . . You men head away now, and let me deal with this. I'll deal with this, okay. You . . . It's important you men don't get in any trouble. So you just scoot, and I'll take care of this."

"Thank you," I say, shaking the good man's hand once more.

He looks at his hand, blood-splattered now. "Better wash up too."

Xan, without words, takes Mr. Wickes's hand and shakes it for a good long time, long enough that we start to hear rumblings back in the alley and Mr. Wickes has to ask for his hand back.

"But you two, you keep it up," he says as we walk. "You do good work. Best of luck, Robert. And Alexander, best, best of luck with the social work course. I knew it. I knew it always."

We walk faster as we exit the alley and see young punks' blood on us. We walk, cool but with purpose, heads down, until we have crested the small Creighton Street hill once again and leave the Dean behind us with one last glance.

Silently Alexander grabs my arm to stop me as he trots over around the side of the mini-mart store. I stand on the sidewalk and watch, puzzled, until he drops to his knees and gets violently, but quietly, sick for several long minutes. I watch him from the sidewalk, and feel the egg growing brand-new on my head.

FIRED/RETIRED

"Which is it, Alexander?"

"What difference does it make?"

I gave him some slack yesterday because of feeling bad for him. He was as sick as a volcano from being so shattered by . . . what? The combination, I suppose. The flashback to the Dean, the trauma of the violence, the blood. And, losing his job. So I backed off, as you do in such circumstances. But also as in such circumstances, it began eating away at me sometime after midnight as I tried to sleep.

But then when I woke up, he was already long gone and stayed gone all day. When he used to go wandering, it was normal day hours and I'd leave for work with him still in bed. When he left early, it was only because of his job. This had the feel of my brother slithering away from me deliberately.

It's my first real shot at him out of Ma's hearing, as we walk to the college for the evening's classes. The ladies are going to meet us out in front of the school.

"The difference," I point out to him, "is that if you quit the only job you seemed able to get, with things being the way they are, I am going to kick your ass. So, do, take your time, and answer carefully."

The last thing I want to do right now is generate any more tension around home. The house feels so heated up already that you can hear the steam hiss as you walk from room to room. But at the same time, lines have to be drawn regarding each individual's behavior, especially when times are toughest.

He sighs heavily. "Robert, it was all strictly on commission. Can you imagine? Me? I didn't make a single dime in the weeks I was there, all right. And I wasn't going to ever make a single dime either, I promise you. It got to the point of being humiliating, just showing up, and I was only doing it after the first two days for Ma and you. So, please . . ."

Not exactly an answer, is it?

"That is not exactly an answer," I tell him, just because I am not quite ready to let it go and I am not prepared with anything more muscular to say.

Truth is, I do feel sorry for him. But you can't do that with Alexander. You can't let yourself feel sorry for him, not obviously anyway, and you surely can't let him feel sorry for himself.

"No, it's not an answer," he says, with just the right bite of defiance in it.

"Hello, hello," I say as we walk up to the two brave lady souls who dare to spend time with us.

"Hello, hello," they say.

Alexander produces a muffled greeting, a look at his shoes, a full blood-orange blush as he makes eye contact with Carly.

Without a tremendous amount of ado, we all head inside to get on with the business of educating ourselves into something like a better life.

"Hey," I say, tugging at Babette before she scoots away toward her own class as Xan and Carly duck into theirs. "Did you get to talk to her about the other night?"

"Yes. She said she had a really sweet time. She said we should all do it again very soon."

"No, I mean about the later stuff. You know, the late-night festivities . . ."

She stares at me now as only Babette has ever stared at me. It is a combination of looks that say simultaneously hurry up and shut up, please elaborate and please no more, jeez you're cute and yet don't touch me.

"Xan never came back from taking Carly home," I answer the silent demand. "Big success. A cause for . . . Oh, now, it wasn't a hate-herself-in-the-morning thing, was it? I hate those. They are *so* unfair. If you can't manage to hate yourself the night before, then you should just keep it to yourself from then—"

"Robert," she says, then checks her watch because we are late now, "he never even walked her all the way home. They were almost there when Alexander said he thought he dropped his wallet in the restaurant, so he left her and ran back."

So irritating. "He never even took his wallet, the cheap—" I interrupt my own thought, with thoughts. "What the hell?" I ask Babette.

"Yeah," she says, "what the hell?"

She kisses me and runs off to class.

What the hell? Staying out all night is not my brother. Staying out with a girl all night is not him either, but that was not him in a good way.

What is this?

I go to my class, but I certainly do not run. And when I get there, I find that my body is in the class but my mind is currently on anything else rather than the theory and practice of high school team sports coaching.

Where is Xan going? With whom? What is he doing with his time? What's he getting at?

The instructor is pointing at me, and my mind is so slow to put words and actions together that by the time I catch what he is saying, all I get is ". . . the other side of the ratio between game theory and teamwork and character development. What say you, Robert?"

I don't even have the mental capacity to offer up a respectable evasion. I stand and collect my stuff as I answer, "I am really sorry, Mr. Melvin, but I have a crashing headache—"

"Yes," he says. "Next time we'll have to send you in your middle-school-floor-hockey helmet." He clearly has not been entirely informed about the circumstances. But my misfortune gets a laugh from the crowd, and that's what's important, after all. "See you next time, Robert," he says.

It is just before break when I hit the hallway and head down the hall toward Social Responsibility. I am standing against the wall opposite the classroom when the door opens. A cross section of cause-conscious society comes rolling out to get their hit of fresh air and cigarettes and dope and very strong coffee and organic oatmeal cookies before resuming the task ten minutes from now of putting everything in the world back right side up. I can almost pick them out, convince myself I can—the PETA person with the llama T-shirt, the anti-warrior in fatigues, the guerilla warrior with the airline captain's cap, the eco-warrior with blond dreads doing the zombie-texting walk. The chubby feed-the-worlder and the no-GM-fooder with the forearm tattoo of Frankenstein's monster holding an ear of corn in each big mitt.

I imagine them all, in turn, getting my brother's shoulder put to their particular wheels. He will feel your pain, folks.

But not before he feels mine.

And then there is beautiful Carly, alone and scowling.

"Where is my brother?" I ask.

"He left after the first ten minutes. With Harry Scary and a few other rough boys."

I immediately pull out my phone and call his number. I have pennies left in my phone, but I already know it is enough for this call as, unsurprisingly, the answer recording picks up in one. That would be because Xan's phone is out of juice, and out of money, and in his sock drawer, where it spends just about all its time.

"Any idea where they went?" I ask.

"All I got was a wave," Carly answers. "They were all slouching and shifting around in their seats when it became obvious we were going to spend a lot of this week's class on boring practical stuff like how to organize an effective targeted letter campaign, lobbying local government, and the basics of non-profit funding."

I think I might be staring at her. I hope not, and if I am, I certainly hope it does not look like leering, because, pretty as she is, it's not that.

It's that she's the real thing.

"I found it very, very informative, myself. They're really missing something."

The real thing.

"Thanks," I say.

"Robert? That Harry gives me chills. He always looks like he wants a fight. And he argues causes in class as if he's itching to start a fight."

"Right," I say.

"And Alexander thinks the guy's, like, a god."

"Wrong," I say. "Very wrong. Thanks, Carly."

I leave her to go back to her class because the real future of the country should not have gaps in her social responsibility résumé. I text Babette to let her know I won't be meeting her after class, and I leave.

I wander around with no idea at all what I might accomplish, where I might hope to find him. I go past the vegetarian restaurant, hoping that maybe that is Harry's command center, or lair, or whatever a guy like him has. The restaurant is less busy than when we were there, so it's easy with one casual stroll through the rooms to see that I won't find them here. The waiter recognizes me, thanks me again for my girlfriend's generosity, though he is too kind to put it that way, and I have a small little breakdown of my normally rock-solid skepticism about people and luck and life.

"Did my brother's wallet ever turn up?" I ask like a dope, like a kid.

He gives me a funny smile and a palms-up shrug. "Your brother did turn up, but I know nothing of his wallet. I presume it was in his pocket."

My attitude joins us again, none too soon, "Or in his sock drawer," I say.

The waiter laughs, and so I laugh with him. That's pretty much it for the evening's laughter.

I just walk. It is, again, not a bad fall evening, clear and cold, the beginnings of wisps of breath playing lightly across purple sky. I walk because walking's not bad, and staying still is, if staying still is even possible right now. I cover ground, my ground, our ground, if we actually have one. All of our living has been done more or less in these streets, even if they seem to be shriveling away from us by the day. It is a neighborhood in decay, which may have a bounce-back the way lots of similar places have. I don't know, never have been able to handicap that kind of thing. Guess that's why I'll never be a real estate or banking success. I don't have that kind of vision. Guess that's why I am going for more the body side of the body-mind area of education. I can make something of that, coaching, teaching, guiding. Not something huge, but something. I can make something there.

And here. I don't mind this neighborhood, assuming it doesn't go any more downhill. I've never felt uncomfortable here. I've always fit nicely. I can see myself fitting nicely for some time to come. I could see myself, with Babette, maybe, and kids, and a job teaching and coaching somewhere nearby and doing some good and not a bad life. I can see myself fitting, if that's the way it goes.

Alexander never fit. Let's be honest. He never fit here. Who knows if he ever would have fit anywhere. That is certainly open to debate, but what is not open to debate is that he never fit here, not as a little kid, and not as whatever the hell he is now.

I pass by the school again, the Dean, through no fault of my own. I have no design as I walk around, ideally to catch up with my brother. In person, as well as the way I am catching up with him now, in my mind.

I should have seen better when we were here at the Dean, and before, and after. I should have watched out. I should have cared.

I walk around, and around, and look in the pizza shop, the Lebanese café, the bar where he would never be served but they would let him play pool. I look down the baseball field where the bleachers are still hot-popular even if baseball itself is as dead as meat around here now.

I walk until I realize I am walking where I have already walked at least twice, and I only notice because the same places are now closed or closing. I walk until it no longer makes sense to walk. Though, if I'm honest, I reached that point a long time ago. But it was still good to keep walking. Now it is time to stop.

The house is dark and quiet, and even the old lock puts up no fight because I finally did show it who was boss with some WD-40 I borrowed from Nick's place. Must remember to return the WD-40.

He is not here, of course, and Ma is long gone to bed. She goes to bed earlier, which is certainly no bad thing, healthy and all, except it seems she is attempting to pull the end of one day ever closer to the beginning of the next, neglecting to search for any of the old small happinesses in the soft-around-the-edges parts of the day that the three of us used to get pleasure from. When we could. It was never a laugh riot around here, but it was nice. Warm. Sane. Unafraid.

Now, seems she wants to work, get the pay, get off her feet, get some oblivion, get up, and get at it again.

That's not a life. Is that a life?

It's only temporary, though. Eyes on the prize and all that. Victory will be that much sweeter.

He is not home. I will wait. We will talk. I will listen, and it will be better. Ma and me and Xan makes three. We will be a formidable thing, when we join our forces together. Divided we fall. That's the thing, isn't it? A house divided against itself, right? We cannot be that anymore. We won't.

I am extremely tired as I lay my head down, but I know, like always, I will sleep aware. When somebody moves in this house, I will know it and I will respond, and when Alexander and I get together and talk, and I listen and he listens, it will be magic. The missing magic. The way deep-in-the-night talk can be.

Who needs a Harry? He has me.

We don't have that talk, because he never does come home.

My alarm goes off too soon, the way it always does. I feel like I just got to sleep, but I am straight up with it for a change and quick to Alexander's bed. I stand there, staring at it, as if demanding an answer.

The bed is unimpressed.

Angrily I just swipe at the bed, tearing away the covers and slinging them to the foot of the bed, to the floor.

And stand there again over the bed, but now standing over the book he had stashed away the other day. I pick it up.

It's a U.S. government manual, *Improvised Explosive Devices*.

You know when everything rushes you, both the world outside and yourself inside, all rushing at the speed of sound, the physical world and the mental whipping circles that take you along with them, like the most insane roller coasters?

That feeling is this. I pick up the book, and stare at it for possibly ten seconds, possibly ten minutes. I do nothing, other than stand staring at the words printed on this thing, I do nothing, but the feeling of motion in all directions is overwhelming, sickening.

"What the hell?" I say out loud before I hear the sound of my mother getting her coffee.

I quickly take the book and shove it out of sight, into my own backpack. Quickly I pull on my grease monkey stuff and join her at the table.

"Is he not up yet?" she says.

I don't attempt a response before the phone rocket goes off, and I see us both jolt rigid with the tension.

"Don't answer it," she says, routine.

"Oh, no," I say, marching toward the phone with all the fury I know. "He picked the wrong morning, truly."

"No," Ma calls. "Please, Robert—"

Too late.

"Right," I spit into the phone, "you looking to *settle*, asshole?

Come right on over. I'll wait for you, and you and I will—"

I am stopped good and sharp, mid-rant. My fury is an instant distant memory as I am shrunk right back down.

I hold out the phone to her, most reluctantly.

"Police," I say.

SHHH, PLEASE

"You have to do something," Alexander says. "You can't just stand by and do nothing."

"I'm going to do something," I say. "I'm going to kill you. How's that?"

Ma is destroyed. After a humiliating full day of our waiting, they released him to her tears and integrity, but they didn't release her from anything. We are on the bus, almost to our stop, when she just goes, "Shhh."

They are sharing the double seat behind me, and I can't help turning around every few seconds to glare at him.

"How stupid? How stupid can you be, Alexander?"

He stares at me blankly, those foolish caramel glasses bothering me more now than ever. "How am I supposed to answer that? Even if I knew how stupid I could be, is there a grading scale that would help me give you the information?"

"If there was a scale, you would bury the needle," I tell him.

"Shhh," she says. "Please. *Please?*"

I turn back toward the front. I listen to the quiet ping-pong of him saying "Sorry" and her saying "Shhh," both as earnestly as they can mean it.

Here's what he got caught doing. He was at the mink farm. He was liberating the minks. He had collected a stink-load of salmon skins and catfish heads and whatever and a plank. He climbed to the top of the tall chain-link fence with the board under his arm and worked the board over the fence and under the razor wire, easing it out so it made a simple and handy climbing structure—sprinting structure, really—for the minks. After cutting the wire and getting himself over, he ran around and opened scores of cages, sprinkling putrid fish bits in his wake like the pied piper of luxury rodents. Then he climbed back over the fence and spread an irresistible rot-feast across the ground just outside in order to make the silky little prisoners mental with fish lust. Then he waited for the mass escape.

Only there wasn't one. People have this notion that pointy, slinky critters like the mink are somehow fiendishly clever, but that is not entirely accurate. Turns out they were only marginally smarter than my brother, and stayed on the wrong side of the fence, just longing for the food. He waited for ages, and they did likewise. As they did not appreciate the boy's efforts, he finally got impatient and started digging.

As he was clawing at the ground—and I do wish I had been there for that part, anyway—one of the minks got it. Alexander was unaware, burrowing away, when the first expensive, vicious little thing made the flip over the fence, fell all the way to the ground, bouncing off Xan's hip and causing them both to scream.

Three or four more of them got the notion and got over before security types came over from the screams and Alexander took off through the woods. While some free minks ate free fish, some guards easily recaptured them.

And one, of course, captured Alexander.

He said he was almost away when they reached him. The stench of fish was the final giveaway as he lay in the leaf cover.

"And you smell like garbage," I say. "It's a wonder they let us on the bus."

"I'm sorry," he says.

"Shush," she says.

It is time for us to get off anyway, and we make the short walk to the house in complete silence.

First up the stairs, I go to unlock the door, and it pushes in easier than ever. WD-40 didn't achieve that.

"Did we leave this unlocked?" I say to her, stepping gingerly into the house.

"I don't know, Robert," she says, giving me a small desperate shove. She just wants to get in and out of sight of the world. "It's entirely possible," she says. "I couldn't tell you for sure what I did this morning, frankly. I may well have forgotten to lock it."

"I'm sorry," Alexander says for the hundredth time.

"You can stop saying that now," she says, heading for the kitchen.

"Really?" I say. "I don't think he can." I walk slowly,

deliberately, around the house, taking it in. Somebody has been in here. I can smell somebody, and it is not us. I can feel the blood rush up into my face. I shudder, like a giant is holding my feet and shaking out my skeleton. This is *our home*.

Ma pours herself a glass of red wine as high as she can pour it and still hope to transport it to the table without incident. She stops before reaching the table.

"I trust this is okay with you, Alexander," she says dryly, holding up the glass.

He just nods.

She takes a big sip as I finish my inspection and just stand behind her. I'm still too agitated to sit, thinking of the guy, walking around *our home*. Looking at our stuff, our lives. Judging. Touching.

"They are calling you a *terrorist*," she says, a renewal of horror flashing across her features. "Do you know that, Son? They are saying you are part of an animal rights activist *terror cell*."

"I'm *not*!" he snaps. "I freed some innocent animals. Where is the terror in that?"

"Then, what do you know about the other stuff?"

The other stuff. Even more creative. At roughly the same time, a bunch of like-minded champions paid a visit to the university, where the animal experiments happen. They did the traditional red/blood spray-painting on the walls, "Murder," and "Torture," the usual suspects, and they pelted the windows with eggs that contained fairly developed embryos, which will make dramatic stains on the glass while possibly conflicting their message. But that was just the prelim. A quarter mile away, a splinter group was working the cemetery in the darkness. Digging away like steam shovels for hell, they were halfway to exhuming the body of the recently departed emeritus head of the biochem lab when a police cruiser turned into the grounds and they scattered like rabbits.

"I had nothing to do with that," he says with the conviction of a criminal.

"She asked what you knew about it."

He stands there. I stand there. Ma sits there. We wait.

"Can I get in the shower?" he finally says. "I really reek. Can I just . . . get this off me?"

"I don't know," I say smartly. "Can you?"

"Yes," she says, "go on."

Ma drinks all that red fast enough that even I get a bit alarmed. Not so fast, though, that I am going to say anything. She goes back to refill, finishes the last of one bottle and screws the top off another. She returns to the table with two full glasses.

I don't really care much for red wine.

"And he's the only one of the whole group that gets caught, of course," she says.

"Of course," I say. I sip my wine. It's full and strong, like Welch's grape juice, the real stuff, with a couple caps of vinegar to kill the sweet. I will never again drink this on purpose.

"He's a good boy, Robert."

"He's an idiot."

She sips.

"I'm getting us some crackers," I say.

I go to the cupboard, and it is not bare. There are crackers.

"It's not his fault," she says, taking a bite of Ritz so small she may be planning to save some of the cracker for leftovers tomorrow.

That is enough for me. I get to my feet, walk to her, and kiss the side of her head. "I am going to make something for dinner," I say. "You just sit."

She gives me no fight, just sits, and sips, and when I bring her the remote, I carefully select a news-free station and she accepts the celebrity cooking program on offer. For company. For pleasant airy nothingness of sound.

There is pasta. And tuna, and a lump of the feta Ma likes to use for a comforting jolt of wine-friendly salt. And frozen spinach. And, there is a meal.

I snap the freezer door closed, and the picture smiles double at me. It has been there for years, all laminated and pristine, and mostly it's there but not there, but at other times, bam. This is bam.

Crisp white shirts; wide, happy smiles. Matching buzz cuts. This was the one year they allowed siblings to take their school photos together. Ma's favorite of all time, and why not? Third and fourth grade, I think we were, and we were straight from the mail-order-good-kids catalog. Alexander is in front and I am right behind, propped with one elbow each on a table, posed and expressing like almost exact twins, and happy about it. Except, of course, I am bigger. I look just slightly older, stronger, surer.

I look protective of him. And he looks protected.

It's a striking, beautiful portrait. The magic of photography.

By the time the TV chef and I have finished our respective duties, there is a meal on the screen and a meal on three plates, and three tired somebodies together around the table for a proper sit-down meal like a family should. There is even wine for three.

The wine for Alexander, it turns out, may be a ploy.

"Please, Ma," he says, "don't ask me anymore. I can't tell anybody who they are."

"You know things will go better for you if you do. You heard them tell us that today."

"I know. I heard. I can't."

"You don't owe those reptiles anything anyway," I snap.

"They are not reptiles. They are people who care about things, and are willing to do something about it."

"People who care," Ma says, low but bitterly serious, "do not desecrate graves."

"I know," Xan says. "I didn't do that. I wouldn't do that."

We descend into that low human sound of just eating, clicking, slurping, not communicating, that happens when the higher human interaction of the communal meal breaks down. Behind us and off to the side a few feet, the TV chefs are in the same stage, but commenting on everything, saying why it is so great—because not a bit of it is ever less than that—and punctuating every thought with mmmms of joy.

"This is really good, Robert," Alexander says while examining the food for visual clues to its taste.

"Wonderful, Robert," Ma says, nearing the bottom third of her bowl, eating more in a sitting than I have seen in weeks.

I am more flattered than I should be, but feeling good feels good, so we go for it. "There's a little more," I say. "Can I get you some more?"

"I could go for a bit more," Alexander says, happy enough, I think, to be part of a normal and civil conversation.

I grab up his bowl, point to Ma's.

"If there was just some bread I could use, to mop up some of this beautiful oil and spinach mixture," she says, and I go look.

I return with Alexander's refill and Ma's perfectly crusty bread that was not quite this perfectly crusty when we got it, and I stand over a table that is as happy as it is likely to be tonight. And I feel I can finally take my own shower.

I slip away and leave them to it, and when the water hits me in the shower, it is first a shock, a small battle against hot needles, then shortly an ease into another welcome relaxing, transforming state. Like acupuncture, I imagine.

From the time of the phone call this morning until now, the day has not been a day at all. I called Nick, who was great about it, though I didn't get too specific and he did remind me to return his WD-40. Then I got out of grease clothes and into respectable meet-the-authorities attire, then took a bus and another bus and a walk that altogether made me feel greasier than if I had worked a double shift at Nick's. Then we sweated at the station for a couple of very unpleasant hours. ("You the angry young man who answered the phone this morning?" "Sorry, sir. I answer that way every time before I've had my coffee.") Then another nasty walk and a couple more sweaty tense bus rides with the addition of the incredible Catfish Kid, and what you have here is the most exquisite shower in the history of water.

It is easily forty minutes before I step out again. And when I do, I walk the walk of the thoroughly-boiled-pasta man. Bed is a fine dream to me now.

I come out to a table that has only one person at it. I walk up behind Ma, take my seat to her right, and point across to Alexander's empty place.

"Where is—," I start to say, then I see her, head on hand, eyes closed, face inclined in the direction of the dream-home-in-the-sun real estate program.

I take up my half glass of wine, which has waited for me, and I sip, and somehow the taste has improved. I lean on the table, on my elbows, getting my face up close to hers. *Are you dreaming this?* I ask her, but only in my head. *Poor mother, are you dreaming of this, this better place, this dream home in the quiet, in the sun, where the sea is clear and turquoise and the sound of it is everywhere and the wind is delivered from the local vineyard to your door by the milkman of dreams?*

"Great," she says, opening her eyes, and I jump enough to make my wine splash fat plum ploplets around the table. "That food was the best I have had in a long time. Thank you, good boy."

"You are entirely welcome," I say. "Where is the bad one?"

"We have no bad ones," she admonishes, finger wag and all.

"The less good?"

"For now," she allows. "And he has gone out." She notices the liftoff of my eyebrows toward space at that, and cuts me off. "Asked if he could go and see Carly for just a little while. I thought that was not a bad idea."

I nod. "The only not-bad idea. In fact, the best idea."

As long as it's true. He's too scared and sorry now for it to be anything else. Right?

MISSION CREEP

Trust is important. Everything spins out of trust.

It's the same every night now. Off to Carly's. Off to Carly's.

A wonderful little love story blossoming there. Something all interested parties should celebrate. Happy for him. Happy for them. Happy for the wider world, which is the truest beneficiary.

Things to celebrate. Love. And trust. I love my brother.

Trust endures into the third night of off to Carly's.

Not having a phone number for Carly, there is only one option. I lie on my bed long enough to be sure my mother has gone to bed. Then I am up and out.

I remember Carly's house from all those times she refused to invite me inside. I feel almost as tentative and awkward pressing the doorbell now as I did back then. This time, though, I will be satisfied with her telling me to go away, once my suspicion is put to bed. And I will smooth over any hurt feelings my brother may have over not being trusted.

"I haven't even heard from him," says Carly, shivering and shifting in her flannel nightgown that brushes the tops of her bare feet. "Why? What's going on? You look worried. Did something happen?"

"Um, well, yeah. I'll let him tell you, though. I'm more concerned right now with making sure something more doesn't happen. He's acting unusual. I want to make sure he's not getting involved in more than he can handle."

"That would be Harry. Harry is more than he can handle, Robert. I even told him, if he's going to keep hanging around with Harry and his *associates*, then I didn't know if I wanted to be seeing him anymore."

"Oh, no," I say, "don't do that. No, Carly, you are a good thing. You're a great thing, even, smart and beautiful and any guy's dream—"

"My, you just never stop trying, do you?"

"I don't mean like that. It's just, don't give up on him that easily."

"That's what Alexander said. He said I didn't understand, but that I would see, and I would get it."

Even when my brother expresses love and hope for the future, it sounds like a threat.

"Just try to be patient with him," I plead. "Right now I think I need to go find him."

"Unfortunately, my guess would be that your best bet is Harry's office."

"His office."

"The restaurant. The back room of Olde City Walls."

"Gotta go, Carly," I say, backing away in a rush.

"I want to know . . . ," she says sternly.

I wave while running for the Olde City Walls.

"Carly, you're looking as lovely as ever," I say. I am standing in the doorway between the main room and the shady back room of the restaurant. There are foolish old hippy beads draped between me and the gathering. Harry and I are eying each other across the distance.

Alexander jumps up so nervously from the cozy table of four that his chair kicks right over backward.

"What are you doing?" he snarls at me through the beads. "You got no business. You are way out of line."

"Hello, Robert. Nice to see you again," Harry calls.

"Hi, Harry. Pleasure's all mine."

Their little round table is set with tiny coffees and larger teas and even small plates of cookies that make it seem like a precious and quaint get-together.

"Don't embarrass me," Alexander growls. "Go home."

"I'm planning to go home. I'm also planning for you to come home."

"Yes, well, you don't plan for me. Get out."

My brother has been hostile with me before, but he hasn't been this. There is a fierceness here I would have sworn he did not possess one week ago, and it's not far off to call him scary.

"Xan," Harry calls, "invite your brother in. Relax, calm down, don't sweat it."

It's as if Harry's words, in Harry's voice, are an audible code that causes Alexander to just do his will. My brother moves aside for me like an automatic door. An automatic door with a scowl.

"Coffee?" Harry asks as I sit across from him, with Alexander to my left. Two guys sit on either side of Harry, but nobody's introducing.

"Not at this time of night, thanks," I say. "It'll keep me awake."

"Cookie?"

I take a cookie, and turn to Alexander. "What are you doing here?"

He looks around the table, then back to me. "Talking to my friends."

"Every night?"

He shrugs.

"So why do you have to lie about it?"

"Because you wouldn't understand."

"What do you talk about?"

"You wouldn't understand."

Harry cuts in. "Maybe you shouldn't assume that, Xan."

"Since I know him," Alexander says, "I think I'll just go ahead and assume."

I turn to Harry. "Coffee would be fine," I say, and his right-hand man pours me some. Time to get serious. "So, you the grave robber, Harry?"

"I didn't rob any grave, no."

"Sorry. So, were you the *attempted* body snatcher?"

He doesn't flinch. "Yes."

I sip my coffee, like I am cool, which I am not. I look to my brother. "And that's okay with you. Is that right, big man?"

Alexander pulls his lips tightly together and shakes his head a slow and emphatic, no.

"No," Harry says. "Your brother did not approve. He couldn't yet see the wisdom of the action. That's why he was sent on assignment elsewhere. Unfortunately, that's also why he got caught. I'll need to keep him closer by me, to keep watch over him in the future."

Like a good brother should.

"And you?" I ask Harry. "You would actually have gone through with that? You would dig up that man's body?"

"He wouldn't feel a thing."

"And do what with it?"

"We were going to put him on the river. Float him right through the heart of the town, carrying our flag. Give him the send-off he deserved. A kind of Viking funeral to highlight all he did for so many other creatures during his life. I am certain the professor wouldn't have minded. Flesh and bone, after all, nothing more."

I turn again to Alexander and see the struggle on his face. But I see he is not giving in without a fight. Not giving in to me, at least.

"Your flag?" I say, hard.

"This is *my* team, Robert," he says, poking himself in the chest hard enough to make a dent. "We care about stuff that is important, and we care enough to do something about it. This—" he gestures in a circular motion around the table—"is important. *I* am important here."

He is getting himself all flustered, and Harry seizes the moment.

"We're known as the Good Causes," he says with some pride.

"Known by whom?" I ask, with some disdain.

"By a select few," he says. "But that will soon change."

It might be the coffee, which is quite strong, but my head is starting to swim. Harry is giving me the smile of a host who is responsible for being diplomatic, but around me there is nothing but dead seriousness, Xan most of all.

"It'll change how?" I ask. "You guys going to go around digging up bodies all over the place? Releasing captive animals? Vandalizing buildings?"

"Yes," Harry says calmly. "Whatever it takes. By any means necessary."

I stand up straight. I look all around at them to see how much of this is bluster, how much is crazy, how much is real.

Alexander, for one, could not look more real.

"I told you you wouldn't understand," he says to me.

"And you were right," I say.

He stands up to address me, man-to-man. "But I really wish you would," he says. "Listen, what we do is, what our aim is, we try to do something to make the world just a small bit better every night. Our goal is to do *something*, every night, to make the world just a bit better, before we allow ourselves to go to sleep. The world needs something, Robert. It's rotten, and it needs a shake."

Alexander himself is shaking. I don't know whether it's fear or anger, or volcanic righteousness bubbling up inside him, but he is in visible turmoil.

"So you shake the world. Then you can sleep comfortably. Is that it?"

He has seized himself into red-faced silence.

"It will be a long time before we can sleep comfortably in the stench of this society," Harry says, "but yes, that is more or less the idea."

"A person has to do something," Alexander blurts. "You can't just not do something."

Is that true? I keep hearing it, but I still don't know if that is true. It might be nice to be certain. It also might be hell.

"So what are you going to do tonight, to make the world just that little bit better?"

My intention is more to be provocative than to actually gain any information. What I provoke, however, is a flurry of looks, exchanged like laser fire this way and that among the eyes of all the Good Causes. Something silently has been communicated, because Harry then says to me, "Why don't you come and see?"

Now it is my turn to get all torqued up. I feel suddenly as nervous as a cat caught in traffic, and all my sureness skitters away.

"I . . . no, not a chance. I didn't come here to . . . You people are out of your . . ."

"You are scared," my brother says approvingly.

"If you had half a brain, you'd be likewise," I say.

"Then I'm glad I don't. Go home, Robert. Let us get on with our business."

"You know what, I will do that," I say, backing away, backing up into and through the absurd hippy beads. "Go make the world a better place, while I go home and sleep peacefully."

"Peace," Harry says.

NIGHT VISION

I don't say anything when Alexander comes in a few nights later, puts on his jacket, and goes out again. I don't say anything now, because I don't say anything much ever. We make a show of it when Ma is in earshot, but otherwise we are on different channels. To hell with him and his Good Causes. He's got his team now, his family. He is no longer my problem. Finally, and good riddance.

"Again?" I hear Ma say to him. His timing is off, and she hasn't gone to bed yet. "Every night, over to Carly's? Aren't you maybe going a little bit fast with this, Alexander?"

"Just going to shoot a little pool, Ma," I say, emerging into the living room and pulling on my own coat.

"Oh," she says, "well, together. That's a nice, strange sight. Haven't seen you two go out together in a while."

"We won't be late," I say, grabbing Alexander stiffly by the arm and aiming him out the door.

"Right," I say as we quick-step down the stairs into the crisp steam-breath air, "so, show me."

Of course he's my problem.

"Can I ask why you didn't go to class tonight?" I ask as we approach Olde City Walls.

"We already learned everything," he says.

"I thought the class was good for you, Alexander. It was *something*, anyway."

I watch his puffs of air, waiting for them to spell something out that makes sense to me.

"I didn't see the point after Mr. Fogerty asked Harry not to come anymore."

"Mr. Fogerty . . . How does anybody get thrown out of social responsibility? What the hell did he do?"

"He didn't do anything. It was a clash of personalities."

I am shaking my head as I speak. "Come on, Alexander. That can't be good. Mr. Fogerty has, like, no rules at all, and Harry managed to break them. You didn't have to stop going just because Harry did. You could be Carly's guest. Why don't you just go back—"

"There will be plenty of time for Carly," he says, discussion-ending serious.

I find myself standing in front of the beads again. I point my finger through them, at Harry.

"Nobody gets hurt," I say.

He points back. "You have my word."

Harry's word. Is that something a person wants to have?

It is only the three of us tonight, and as the team emerges back out into the night, I catch Alexander making the switch. Off come the caramel-colored protectors of the soul windows, and out come the old glasses, clear-lensed and exposed.

"I see," I say. "Night vision goggles. I was wondering how you managed these conditions. I thought maybe you had developed bat skills."

"I wish," he says solemnly.

Bat skills or night goggles, he would need something as the three of us wend our way silently through the darkest streets of the town. We take no main routes, we talk no more than necessary. We are never far from the more sensible, straight A-to-B desire lines of city traffic, but just off the beaten track. We are like a three-headed stalking horse of the town's regular folk one block over.

And something about it is immediately thrilling.

Maybe I will be convinced. Maybe we will actually achieve something in our own small way that will make the world a better place. I get a rush thinking about it, and thinking about the possible dangers as well.

"What are we doing?" I ask Alexander as we approach the county hospital.

"We are visiting the doctor."

"What doctor?"

"Dr. Griffin," Harry says as we slip into the poorly lit parking lot of the hospital. It is a small operation and, frankly, tired. Hardly a week goes by when our old County General isn't brought up in the news for the neglected sad pile of a hospital it is. There are proposals to modernize it. There are always proposals.

Harry hops onto the hood of a classic and well-preserved cream-colored BMW 320i. License plate says DRGMD. "Do you know of Dr. Griffin?"

"Sounds familiar," I say, "but I am not sure why."

"The why is, the good doctor was in the news last week for refusing to check a patient in because he thought he was an illegal alien."

"Right," I say, "now I know. The guy's appendix burst. And he died . . ." I look around.

"Right over there," Harry says, pointing to an alleyway with a couple of Dumpsters in it.

"Was he illegal?" Alexander asks.

"Yes," Harry says. "He used the name and social security number he got off some prison inmate in Virginia to get ID and medical attention all over, but so what? What did Dr. Shithead care? It was none of his business. He was way out of line. There was a person who needed a doctor, that's all that mattered."

Harry, working up an anger, starts bouncing the car a little.

"So, what are you going to do, bring the guy back?" I ask.

"That would make the world a little bit better, no doubt," Alexander says.

"No doubt," Harry says. "But since that's not possible, we are just going to have to make the world better by reuniting Dr. Griffin with his humanity. We'll be sort of like the three ghosts visiting Dr. Scrooge."

Harry hops down off the car. He reaches into his inside pocket and pulls out a bottle of water and a badge. The badge is a hospital ID.

"Where'd you get that?" I ask as he clips it to his jacket.

"This is where I did my volunteer gig for Jerk Fogerty's class. I did the half day for the class, and then decided to stay longer. I pushed the newspaper cart all over the building for a couple of weeks, got to know the place really intimately. Then just kept the badge. It's just for volunteers, but nobody around this sorry place really looks closely."

"Okay. What do we do?" Alexander asks, agitated now.

Harry hands him a six-inch stainless steel screw. "While you are engraving our message into this creamy hood, 'Basic health equals a Good Cause,' I will be visiting the doctor's office. This"—he shakes the water bottle—"is the doctor's brand, always at his side. But this blend is a bit special, and will help him be more humane, at least for this one night, as he sees emergency patients."

Now it's different. I was nervous until now, but the heat just went way up inside me. My chest pounds.

"You gave me your word, no one would get hurt."

"And no one will."

I am startled by an awful metallic scratch noise. Alexander is already carving the hood.

"And off we go," Harry says, backing toward the hospital. "When I come back down, we'll head around to the front, to emergency. One of us will say we need treatment, so we can check on our man."

"Brilliant," Alexander says, demented-sounding.

"Insane," I say.

"Not at all," Harry says, trotting now. "The ends will justify, and you will see. You just don't leave your brother exposed. Let him know if anyone's coming."

"Yeah," Alexander says, "you got my back, Robert. You got my back?"

I sigh nervously, look all around, nervously.

"I got your back," I say.

It is a solid twenty minutes before Harry returns. The message has been finished for a while, and we squat, low and invisible on the ground beside the car. Harry runs right up to us, buzzing with excitement.

"It took me forever to be able to switch the bottles. First his office was locked. So then I went to the news storage, grabbed a few papers, and went right down to emergency, like I was delivering papers. There he was, being cold and nasty to the city's less fortunate, so like a three-card monte dealer I switched the bottles so smooth nobody could ever tell, even though I did it right under his nose. I even offered him a paper, but he told me to get out of his damn way, he didn't want a damn paper. Oh, well."

"What's in the water, Harry?" I ask grimly.

"It's sort of plant food. Plant food that makes love bloom in the human heart. Right about now he should be feeling it big-time, for his fellow travelers."

"And what is that?" I ask, pointing to what looks like a giant lunch box hanging from his hand.

"Toxic medical waste," he says, nodding and grinning joyfully. "This is truly a sorry example of a facility."

Without another word Harry walks to the BMW's driver's door, withdraws a wire from his pocket, and the door is open quicker than if he had the keys. I don't think it was beginner's luck.

I watch in silent horror as Harry dumps old hypodermic needles, various plastic bottles, soiled bits of gauze, and whatnot all over the front seat of the car.

"Now not only will he relocate his humanity, he won't ever forget it again either."

"Yes!" Alexander says, bouncing up and down like a fighter approaching the ring. "Yes! Right. Too right, Harry."

"Wrong," I say. "Wrong."

Harry is unfazed by doubt—mine, his, or anyone else's. "You will see in the end, my brother."

"Yes, my brother," my brother says, "you will see."

"Right," Harry says. "It's off to emergency—"

"Hey!" comes the bellow across the lot. Even Harry is jolted with the shock.

We turn to see a man in a white lab coat running—staggering, really—our way. "What are you doing to my car?" he shouts, and runs a few more steps before veering crazily sideways and crashing headlong onto another parked car. The crunch as he slams into the fender resonates all over, and it sounds like the car has hit him rather than vice versa.

"What are you doing?" Harry says, grabbing Alexander's arm as he lurches toward the doctor. "Are you out of your mind? Let's go." He pulls my brother roughly as they rumble along.

Alexander looks over his shoulder. "Come on, Robert," he calls. "Come on."

I just stare after them for a few seconds, then turn the other way to see the doctor pull himself up to standing, using the hood of the other car to steady himself. He stands there, looking down, with hands flat on the hood. He tries to look up and toward me, but that effort alone seems to defeat him. He makes a small howl of a noise, his head suddenly shaking like someone with Parkinson's. He looks down at the hood once more, wobbles, calls out but forms no words. He topples over onto the hood of the car, landing on his shoulder and the side of his face as if that one arm just completely quit working for him. He looks like a dying animal.

I go to him.

Briefly, just very briefly, as I stand over the writhing, disoriented doctor who has slid right back down to the ground, I think about it. I look over to where the immigrant man lost all. Where his appendix exploded and his life oozed away in the cold shadow of the County General Dumpster.

"They have a point, you know." I am surprised to hear myself say it out loud. They are wrong, but they have a point.

The doctor does not appear to hear me as he works to get himself back up once more. I reach down and grab him firmly by the arm, and around his waist.

"Who are you?" he asks, focusing briefly on me before looking at the ground again. "Are you one of them?"

"No, sir," I say, steering him back toward the building. "I am not one of them."

"Where did they go? Did you see them? What has happened to me?"

"I didn't see anyone," I say. I go through the open door, supporting most of the weight, and follow signs for emergency. "You had a fall. Hit your head."

"Punks," he says, shaking his head hard to try to dislodge whatever mystery bug has gotten in there. "Losers, scumbags.

It's nonstop around here. Don't know why I bother. Lowlifes. You can't help them. They're born in the gutter, and they should just die there. This is the thanks I get."

"It is," I say as we enter the waiting area. Seeing us, a nurse comes rushing from behind the admittance desk.

"What happened?" she asks, taking the doctor's other arm and directing us to one of the assessment cubicles. We lay him down on the cot.

"He fell, hit his head, I think."

She looks worried. Presses a button on the wall for more troops as she looks into the doctor's darting, unfocused, dilated eyes.

"What are you doing?" he asks her.

"I am examining you," she answers.

"Get me an actual doctor. Right now."

Another nurse and what looks like an actual doctor come rushing in and get busy on Dr. Griffin.

I take the opportunity to make my exit.

"I will need to talk to you," the first nurse says. "Don't go away."

"I'll be right out here in the waiting area," I say.

I will like hell. I put my head down and make a quick, inconspicuous beeline for the exit.

COLLATERAL DAMAGE

Harry was right about one thing: the name of the Good Causes is making itself known. Someone managed to spray-paint it in their trademark red letters on the front of the police station one night. I've seen it on the side of a bus and on a billboard that was promoting youth-restoring face cream. It's even turned up on the headstone of the professor they wanted to dig up, just in case anybody thought they had forgotten about him.

"It's nothing too destructive, though, right?" Babette says as we walk to the college for class. I haven't told her about my tag-along mission. Yet. I will tell her.

"They haven't killed anybody, anyway."

"See, that's good."

"I just worry about where it goes from here, how far they are willing to go."

"Not far, is my guess. Robert, as weird and misfitty as Alexander can be, I don't think there is any real malice in him at all. This is all probably just a phase, to make himself feel a little bit powerful, and pretty soon he will back off and find something more constructive to occupy his time."

I look over at her, as we keep walking.

"Pretty in-depth analysis," I say.

She shrugs. "Hey, I am a highly trained student . . . of ecotourism."

Then she stops short.

"What?" I ask.

She points. At the front doors of the college. The new front doors of the gleaming and hopeful community college of our modest, struggling town.

Painted in gleaming red, it says: EDUCATION FOR ALL . . . IS A GOOD CAUSE.

Babette and I continue on to the doors, which we find locked. There is a notice posted in the window, *All classes canceled for today for security purposes.*

"Because poor hapless Harry was put out of class?" I scream at Alexander. "That is reason to vandalize the school and threaten a teacher and disrupt lives all over the place?" I am throwing things. My books. My sweatshirt. Most of my available things are on his side of the room now. I march over and retrieve them just to heave them back to my side.

He does not quite have the zeal of the converted as he defends the Good Causes' position on this. "It was completely unfair, throwing Harry out of the class. They were just trying to silence him, and that is not right. He has rights, same as Mr. Fogerty or anyone else. And it wasn't a threat. It was a reminder, about freedom of speech and the true mission of institutions of higher—"

"Bullshit!" I shout. "You sound like a Harry mouthpiece. This is all about your fearless leader pitching a temper tantrum. Come on, Alexander. You are smarter than this, dammit. I mean, you're a moron, but you are smarter than this."

He stares at me blankly, and picks up his jacket. "You are wrong," he says. "These things matter, Robert. And if people like us don't stand up for things like freedom of expression, then we will all wind up silenced, by government or corporations—"

"Or the friggin' community college?"

"Yes," he says, pointing at me. "The way I see it, we are fighting your battles for you."

"Yeah? Well, don't!"

"You'll see," he says, giving me the brush-off wave as he opens the door.

"You are not actually going out there, *causing* more *goodness* tonight."

"Why wouldn't I? The society is just as rancid as it was yesterday. So we keep up the fight. Just a little bit better every night, remember?"

"Better? Like what you did to Dr. Griffin?"

He visibly flinches, as I strike a bruise. "I didn't do that . . . and he was, is, an awful man."

"If you are planning to erase all the awful men, you're going to be awfully busy the rest of your life."

"I have to go."

"Go," I say. "Go. I hope you have a big night. I wish you the very best."

He is walking, but looking back at me with a look of real worry, like I just made something bad happen.

Because I am not my brother's keeper, I sleep soundly. I don't know how long he crusades into the night, and I don't know what time he comes in.

I have no idea how long he has been at it, when I become aware of the crying.

He is in his bed, crying, sobbing like the little boy he is. I feel transported, back in time, back into the long nights of his under-happy boyhood. I am remembering what I did not even remember, which is how common this was, all those nights all those years ago.

I didn't help him then. I'll have to live with that.

I'm not helping him now. I can live with this.

I roll over in his direction.

"So, Alexander, is the world a better place tonight?"

He cries harder, but it gets softer, muffled as he smothers himself into his pillow.

I roll back over.

TERROR EYES

It is the phone that wakes me up this morning, shrieking, shrill like never before, like no phone ever before, like no phone was ever made for.

I was in such a deep sleep that the shock is insane, diabolical, and it keeps shocking because I am having trouble even getting my bearings regarding where, and when.

I slept like sleeping in a crypt once the blubbering finally stopped.

It keeps ringing. It is barely light out, and I am stumbling around the room. It sounds like it is in the room, but it is not.

The reason it is still almost dark is that it is supposed to be. The sky is doing what it is supposed to do, because the phone is doing what it is not. He is ringing before dawn. He is terrorizing the respite hours now.

The phone rings, and it must be for the twenty-fifth time, and I swear it is getting louder on its own.

I don't hear myself make a sound, but I feel it, a deep and subhuman growl that shakes me and the house and is meant to carry a large ball of fury out of me, through the windows and into the world that deserves it.

"What the hell!" comes the voice, from there, from right there on Alexander's bed, where he was sleeping certainly as deeply as I was. He is sitting up now, and really, I feel like he shouldn't be. I am the man of this house, I am the watcher, the listener, the presence, and he is the boy, the watch*ee*.

The phone must be on ring number forty. I hurdle right over Alexander and his bed and burst through the door, beelining for the phone, ready for this, more than ready for this because this should not be allowed to happen. It should not have been allowed to happen to here, which is why it needs to be undone now and for good.

"No," Ma says, spooking me. She is standing there in bluish morning light, in her bluish-whitish nightgown in the light of the front window, standing in front of the phone.

"I want to handle this, Ma," I say.

"And I want you not to. I will handle it, when I can. That's not now. Go back to your room. You have time."

"Then shut off the ringer. Just for now," I say, because she has always freakishly refused to cut us off. "Landline is lifeline" she has said since the one and only time she was disconnected by the phone company.

"Just for now, Ma," I insist.

"For now," she says, clearly the controller at this point. "Until you calm down."

I turn right away from her. I can't be like this. I need to be the controller. *Get your shit together, Robert,* I say to myself as I re-enter the bedroom and pull the door behind me.

"What's happening, Robert?"

His voice, at this instant, is no better than the screeching phone in my head.

"What's happening? Hard-guy? What's happening, you ask?" I climb right onto his bed, sit right on his solar plexus, just like the good old days.

"Robert," he says nervously but without struggle, "cut it out, man. You're freaking me out."

"Freaking you out?" I say, leaning way down close and breathing hot into his face. "How can that happen, hard-man? Nobody freaks out the terrorist. It's the terrorist that freaks everybody else."

"Don't call me that. Stop calling me that. I'm not a terrorist of any kind, and you know it."

I shake him. I shift, getting my knees up onto his chest. I dig my knees into him.

"Robert!" he says, coughing, wheezing. I jolt him harder. "What is wrong with you? I haven't done anything."

"Sure you have," I say. "You've done plenty of things, lots of things. You just haven't done any of the right things. While you are out there with your big scary friends, saving little furry animals and making the world safe from everything but yourselves, we have our own terrorist right here, terrorizing us. Terrorizing *Ma,* Alexander the Terrorist."

"Don't call me that," he insists, still wheezy. "I am not that."

"Oh, really?" I say, jumping off with an extra dig into his ribs.

I hop into the space between the two beds, and he reaches onto the night table and puts on his stupid butterscotch glasses.

"So what is this?" I say, grabbing my backpack from the floor so I can show him the book I stashed there when I found it. He hasn't even had the guts to inquire since I stole it.

"No, Robert!" he shouts. "That's mine. Leave it alone!"

"It's mine," I answer, and then notice I am wrong. I have grabbed his backpack, which is practically the same. I look at the backpack, then back at him, his terror-stricken face, and I wonder. "What is it, Xan? What am I going to find in here? I wasn't even interested in your backpack. Till now."

I tear it open before he can grab it from me. I reach in.

Oh. This explains it.

"Would this explain it, Alexander?"

I hold in my hand a contraption, the size of an extra large deodorant can. It is cold, with wires at either end and electrical tape all around it. There is putty of some kind at the wire bits, like they are little vines growing there.

I hold it in my hand, and stare at him.

He is up on one elbow. He looks down at the floor.

"I was just going to get rid of it, Robert, I swear. I was never going to use it. It was never my idea."

He won't raise his head. I lay the demonic little device down on my bed, then turn back to my brother.

"Look at me," I say evenly.

Slowly he raises his face to me. The first of the sun comes through the window and lights up his glasses.

"Take those *goddamn* things off," I say, and in possibly the most truly violent act of my life, I belt Alexander so hard across the face that the glasses fly on their own, right off his skull and smack into the wall. He covers up, but it's pointless. "Come here," I say, grabbing hard all the hair at the top of his head. I can feel his scalp shift as he moans and I drag him, off the bed, across the floor, right up to the mirror.

That is, *right* up to the mirror. I take his face and I press it viciously up to the glass.

"You see this? Huh? Do you see this, Alexander?"

"Of course I see it," he says, real fear now. Good, the real fear. "It's me, for crying out loud."

"Good guess. Now, tough guy, world-beater, look closer. You see? You see, those soul windows? You see?"

"I see!" he says desperately.

"You do. You do see. You see just what I see, right? Do you see a killer in there? Do you see something brutal there? No! No! What you see there is a big-eyed baby seal! That is who you are."

"I am not!"

"Yes, you are, and that is good. Leave it alone! You don't have the balls for it. If you had any guts at all, you wouldn't be out there trotting at the heels of psychotic Harry and settling his scores. You would be here doing something serious to the *bastard* problem your own mother has." I am bouncing his face off the mirror now, punishing the shark bill collector with my poor brother's face. "You know what I would do right now if I could find that sonofabitch—"

He sniffles.

"You can find him," Alexander says.

I instantly stop. I still grip his hair tightly, but all motion stops. I look at the two of us in that mirror, me right behind him, me right above him. There is a thin trickle of blood coming from his nose.

We look like a sickened, degraded version of the timeless gap-toothed-good-boys school picture hanging on the fridge.

"How do you know where to find him?"

"I know the building where he works."

"And how do you know that?"

"I worked in the same building."

We both let that hang in the air for a minute. Then I feel such a revving inside me, there is no resisting it, no way.

"Get dressed," I say. "We're going to go make the world a little bit better."

"Okay, Robert," he says, still frozen. "I will do whatever you want me to do, whatever you say. . . . But I also think you should take a look at your own eyes right now."

I choose not to.

We talk, and walk with a sense of purpose.

"It's a rancid old cube of filth of a building," Xan says, "filled with all these tiny little maggoty bottom-feeder businesses like third-party bill collectors and repo men and private investigators, who by the way are nothing at all like they show in the movies. And if you didn't know better, you would figure the place was an old storage facility, one that closed for business in the seventies."

"Right," I say, "and what the hell were you doing there? Selling cleaning products?"

He sighs. Not for the first time I have struck the shame nerve.

"I was doing the same thing the Shark is doing."

"Alexander!"

"I know, I know. Not the same, but the same. I worked for this little rat-ass company that rented things—TVs, washing machines, fridges, and all that—to folks who couldn't afford to buy them. By the time their names got to me, they couldn't afford to rent them either. So my job was to bother them for money until they cried."

"Shit, Alexander."

"Shit Alexander, that is exactly who I was. Never made a nickel, of course, because I didn't have the balls for this either."

"Make anybody cry?"

"No, and here's the best part. I finally lost the job when the boss came by and I was on the phone with this lady who had, like, twenty kids under the age of three and one leg and was going to kill herself if she couldn't keep her washing machine, which she needed for obvious reasons—"

"Obvious."

"And by the time the boss—a prince of a guy, by the way—comes by the desk, the lady has *me* bawling like I'm one of her babies. He fires me on the spot."

It is actually a deliriously welcome feeling when the two of us burst out laughing at Alexander's great bad fortune. It goes on for a couple of minutes before I speak.

"You've always been a crier," I say.

"You noticed."

"Sorry about your nose," I say.

He waits, for more, apparently. "And my hair. And the glasses slap . . ."

I look over at his glasses, bent now and slightly skewed. "Yeah," I say. "All that."

We walk, and we walk, to an area of town just as wonderful as Alexander described it. It's not far from Nick's garage, but the two-block difference is the same small difference between having your parachute open, and not.

"How much can this thing do?" I ask, finally broaching the subject that now makes me nervous just thinking about.

"'A righteous boom,' is how Harry describes it. From what I understand," Alexander says, "if properly placed, it basically makes a car not worth fixing."

"Or jacks up a small office?"

"Or that."

We reach the building, stand outside. From the spot where we stand you cannot see a single thing growing. Not a scrub of a tree, not a patch of grass. The river is the closest thing to a thing of nature, a sad little brown slurp passing under the footbridge between this neighborhood and life.

"You sure you want to do this?" he asks me.

"How does it work?"

"I twist a couple of wires together. Then there's a button I push in at one end, and we have five minutes to run like hell."

The two of us jump back when the main door punches open. A short fat guy with seven o'clock shadow and a salmon-colored suit stares at us ignorantly, like he doesn't think he can be seen, then walks on past.

"Absolutely," I say.

"You know, Robert, you might want to smack me again for this, but I have to say, I don't think you're a killer either."

He winces a little, actually anticipating a smack.

I shrug. "Let's go find out."

I stomp into the building, follow Xan's directions to the third and final floor, make a right to the last door.

"It probably wouldn't even kill," he says, hopefully. "Maybe just maim a little . . ."

"Ooohh," I say, "corner office, very impressive."

I march right up, and throw open the door without knocking.

The Shark is sitting there, behind the exact same awful green metal desk I remember from the janitor's room in the basement of the Dean. He is hunched over a stack of papers, and is eating a bacon sandwich with the fatty bits wiggling live like worms through the crust. He does not look up, he does not look surprised. This, apparently, is not an unusual occurrence for him.

"Can I help you?"

"Yeah," I say. "You can stop terrorizing our mother."

He looks up. He just chews.

"Were you in our house, you creepy fat reptile?"

"You should lock your doors," he says. "You should always lock your doors."

He looks back at the paperwork that is clearly of more significance than we are.

"Did you take anything?" Alexander asks, in the unhelpful voice of a hurt little boy.

The Shark looks up again, shoves the remainder of the bacon sandwich—which really should take three bites—into his mouth.

"Listen, boys," he muffles. "Now, I don't mean any offense by this, but the kind of stuff you got, if you tried to give it to me, I'd give it back."

We both slip off our backpacks, walk forward, and take the two seats that sit across the desk from him. They too are that industrial polished metal, and with pea green vinyl seats. They stink like ammonia. The whole place stinks like ammonia.

"Maybe we could give him something now," I say to Alexander.

"Something he wouldn't give back," Xan says. He's putting on a good show, but I can see him trembling. I look down at the packs at our feet, and I see my own knees trembling.

The Shark leans his elbows on his desk, threads the fingers of both hands together, and rests his blunt, stubbled chin there.

"Oh, are you boys threatening to get tough with me? Ah, your mommy must be so proud. Listen, what do you think is going to happen here? You think you can somehow make me stop collecting a bill that has to be collected? Well, that's not gonna happen, all right? People like your mother, who don't pay their bills, wind up with people like me, who help them to do so. So you just go home, and you tell your mom to get herself a second job, or embark on a crime spree, or whatever she has to do, because now that I know that there ain't nothing in your house worth anything other than her pay slip—by the way, which really shouldn't be left lying on the telephone table where any old body can see it—now that I have all that information, you tell your mom my next stop is to come and visit her at work, and get to know all her associates, so she had better come up with something for me, and she better start answering the damn phone, because I ain't going nowhere, understand? So now, get outta my office before I kick both of your asses just to make this job worth my while."

At this point, really, there is no more consultation necessary. The Shark has his sneer of contempt locked on me, and I absorb it while out of the corner of my eye I see Alexander smoothly remove the device from his pack. He twists wires. He makes like he's dropped something, and stands the deodorant can up tucked just inside the thick front leg of the awful desk.

Then he stands up like a shot.

"Come on, Robert," he says with a trembling voice, "let's not get our asses kicked."

He grabs my shirt and yanks really hard, and we are flying, out of the maggoty office, down the maggoty stairwell. I cannot feel my legs under me, I am so wired, with fear, with terror.

"Bye now, momma's boys. I will see you real soon, I'm sure."

I can't even formulate a snappy response, even knowing what I know while the Shark knows not.

I am getting sick to my stomach as we reach the next landing. My system has opened up and released all my body's adrenaline at once, and it feels like it could kill me right on these steps.

"My God," I say as we run. "My God, my God. Xan, what am I doing? My God, Xan. What the hell?"

We keep running, and we hit the ground floor.

I grab my brother by the shirt and yank him to me.

"Xan?" I shout. "What have I done? No way, no way . . . !"

He looks me in the eye really, really hard, focused—sure, like I should be. Then he slaps my hands off him.

And runs.

Like a cheetah.

Back up the stairs.

"Alexander!" I yell, and chase after him. He is well ahead of me, but I am halfway up the third flight when I hear him burst into the Shark's office.

"Oh, Christ, what now?" says the Shark.

"Kick my ass!" Alexander demands.

"What?"

"Come on, ya fat tub. I said, come on. You think you're man enough, come kick my ass."

The Shark says nothing for a second, then, just as I come up on them, Xan runs out of patience. He lunges across the desk, spits heavy in the guy's face, then slaps him hard enough to send the slappy echo all the way down the stairs.

And we are off, to the races once more, Alexander and me flying three steps at a go, and the Shark rumbling hard after us.

When we burst through the door, we continue right across to the other side of the street. Once there, we turn around to find the Shark out of breath and glowering blood-brilliant eyes at us as he rolls up his sleeves and flexes his fists.

The sound is a little underwhelming compared to expectations, but not insignificant.

BU-HOOOM!

It is like a large shotgun blast rather than a bomb, but it is quite a thing, all the same. The two windows of the top corner maggoty office blow right out, glass raining down onto the empty sidewalk. The pile of papers he was working on gets sucked right out the windows, and the devil's deals of a hundred poor saps like us go floating and fluttering all over the neighborhood.

The three of us stand there, staring in amazement. The first judder of awe wears off quickly as I hear the low rut of growl start up in the Shark's throat. I feel like bolting, but I am paralyzed in this spot.

"Oh," the Shark says, with Satan for sure in his voice, "I know who did this. Oh, I know exactly which rotten criminal lowlife did this. Thinks I don't know? Thinks I'm scared off by this kind of . . ."

He marches across the street, to an ugly big ten-year-old white Cadillac parked on the corner. He gets in without even seeming to remember why he was on the street in the first place, and squeals the tires as he heads anxiously to his assignment.

My brother and I stand, stunned, there on the sidewalk, watching the last of the papers flutter to the pavement. We look at each other. Still, words don't come out.

We start walking.

As we cross the footbridge back to life, I reach into my backpack, the right one this time, and pull out the copy of *Improvised Explosive Devices*. As we walk, I dangle the book over the side of the bridge, and let it drop into the thick burbling brown goop of the river, which will certainly dissolve it before we even get home.

"We nearly did the worst thing of all time," I say. "Thanks for having the guts to do what you did. You just made the world a little bit better."

"I'm just glad I got the chance to spit at him," he says.

SOCIAL WORK

Alexander got community service for the mink incident. They never did connect him to the university or cemetery stuff or anything else before his retirement from the Good Causes. If they had, things could have been very different.

As for the other thing.

"Organized crime?" Alexander says when I very quietly read him the local paper account of the explosion. Because that building has something go *boom* about once every three months, there doesn't appear to be a lot of urgency around the inquiries. "For one thing, there was very little 'organized' about it. And for another, whose explosive device are they calling *crude*?"

But all joking aside.

"I know," I say to him when he reminds me how lucky we are.

"And even that, even that word, 'lucky,' is nowhere near strong enough."

"I know," I say.

"We should be both dead *and* in jail, you know that?"

"I know," I say. "We are both very lucky guys."

The phone has stopped ringing. Not entirely, of course, but it has stopped ringing *in that way*. Haven't seen the Shark, here, nor at Ma's work. It's nice, but we know it's not permanent. As soon as he's done a little straightening up, he'll be back.

But we'll be ready. There are three incomes now—if you include a little under-the-table pocket money my brother gets from Mr. Wickes—and no nonsense, and every night we have a good proper family meal and the three of us tally the day's pennies. On Fridays we even have dinner for five. Ma looks very lifelike on Fridays. The other two ladies look hot.

I paused school, but only till the spring semester. Nick found some charity hours for me, and I'm all work and no play for the next few months. Then I can get back to class, with my Babette, and my brother.

He's not going back to *that* class. That's over for him. He's back in January, like me. Full-time, like me, once he finishes off the GED, which frankly he could have passed when he was a freshman.

He's not supposed to be getting paid for his community service. But service cuts both ways in a half-decent community, with fully decent middle school administrators.

"Social work," Mr. Wickes says when I drop off Alexander to begin paying his debt to society. "I knew it. I always knew it."

Alexander turns to me with a completely false *Help me* look, and a completely genuine grin. Then he turns back to Mr. Wickes.

"You know what I don't like?" Mr. Wickes says.

"What?" Alexander says.

"These." And with that he swipes the golden glasses, the guardians of the soul windows, right off the boy's face. "There you are, Alexander," he says happily. "There. Now I can see you in there."

"But I can't really see, sir," Xan says, following Mr. Wickes semi-blindly toward the office.

"Ah, you'll be fine," he says. "It's more important for me to see in than for you to see out. Sometimes seeing everything just gets in the way anyway."

And there the two of them disappear into the office, then reappear again at the big glass partition. Mr. Wickes waves at me, and I wave back.

Alexander waves at somewhere about six feet to the right of me. Mr. Wickes adjusts him, and the boy waves at the actual me.

You've got to do something, right? You can't just not do something.

I wave back at the boy, turn, and head out into a world that is just a little bit better.

Here's a sneak peek at Chris Lynch's next book
PIECES

PHILOSOPHY

My brother is a philosopher. I know this because he's told me, countless times. More than just a philosopher, even.

"Philoso-raptor," he calls himself. "Swift of mind, rapaciously inquisitive." On his twentieth birthday this year he alerted me to the fact that "at approximately two dumps a day, more than seven hundred a year, times twenty years, that puts me over the fourteen-thousand mark for squatting, most of it on the toilet. That, my man, is a lot of contemplation."

That's my brother.

He's always telling me to be philosophical, to take things philosophically. I've never entirely wrapped my mind around what that means, but it seems right now is as good a time as there ever will be to figure that out.

There's a moss-green river that cuts in half just in time to bypass the hospital on both sides. Sometimes it doesn't appear green, but even at those times it smells green. Doesn't matter, though. People are always on the banks, walking up and down, sitting in the park that belongs half to the hospital, half to the river. Because of the sound. It's millions of splashy voices all going at once, and this river is never, ever silent.

I'm standing with my back to the voices and my front to the gleam of the new hospital wing rising up, eight stories of yellow brick and glass against the deep purple clouded sky. I think I've picked out the window on the second floor, in the room where my brother is not going to die. All the voices behind me say that Duane's not going to die.

Is it being philosophical to believe the voices? I suppose it could be.

Is it being philosophical to be picking up golf-ball-size rocks and whipping them one after another at that window like a spoiled and angry and petulant kid?

Of course it isn't. I'm sorry, Duane. I'm sorry, man. You're not even gone and already I'm letting you down.

HARVEST

"No."

"Eric, what do you mean, no?"

Everyone is speaking in hushed tones, which is what you do. The room is too hot, but it is cold death itself. All bald walls and machines, this room is the opposite of humanity. It's all been so fast, there isn't even a card or a flower anywhere yet.

"I mean no, Ma. Nobody's turning anything off."

"Eric," Dad cuts in, and now I couldn't care less.

"Shut it," I say to him, holding up a *Shush* finger, but holding it with my arm fully extended between me and him.

My dad's red-rimmed eyes go altogether wide, but some miracle does in fact shut his mouth. I don't know what I would do if he snapped back at me, or what he would do about what I would do. Everybody's best not finding out, that's for certain.

Ma's face is the exact shade of her pink roses, which she loves more than anything else on God's earth and almost as much as she does God himself. Her cheeks are as wet as if she'd just been sprayed with a spritzer. When she talks, though, she doesn't sound like she's been crying because that isn't her. Not even now. Moisture appears, without tears, like morning dew.

"We have to decide this together," she says.

"No, we don't," I say. "We haven't been *together* on anything since I was twelve, so we're surely not gonna start here."

"Eric," Dad tries, and this time I don't even give him words. He gets that *shush*-finger warning once more, and I speak to Ma.

"It's too soon for anything like this, Ma. Way too soon."

Her hands are prayer-folded, like they are every morning with her rosary beads. "Son, I know you don't want to hear this—"

"You *know* I don't want to hear it, Mother Superior," I say, to insult her piety as much as to make my point, "and yet, I still hear you talking."

I had already made it clear that I didn't want to hear *this*, when *this* first came up a half hour ago and I stormed out of the room and the hospital and the situation. The doctor had his ideas and his procedures and all that, but I had mine. My solution was to throw rocks. From what I can tell, I've done as much good as he has.

I am seventeen years old. Or I was, before my big shitslice of a brother went diving into the quarry and broke his neck and his skull and my grip on the world. Now I'm about seven.

Full credit to Ma, she's not fazed by me, and she's not blinking from what remains of Duane. Almost wish I had religion now. She makes it look useful.

"He's not getting any better, Eric," she says, almost serenely.

"And he's not going to."

I fight an impulse. I fight and I fight and I fight it, and I don't know what it looks like on the outside but inside I am thrashing and punching and clawing at this thing, because while I am not great at impulse fighting, I know this is the right battle.

So, you and Dad aren't getting any better either, but we're letting you live.

That's what the impulse wants to say. But even I know this is wrong. Even now, even I.

I think Duane-ish instead.

"If there is one thing I know in this world, then this is the thing I know," I say, echoing one of my brother's catchiest catchphrases. "Duane belongs to me a hell of a lot more than he belongs to you. This decision is *mine*."

At seventeen years old I know this decision is not mine. But there's knowing, and there's knowing.

The discussion is over.

"I want some time," I say to them. "We need some time. He told me," I say, pointing beside me to the bandaged and purpled, ventilated hissing husk that is my brother. "We need some time alone. Can we have that?"

Who could say no to that? The only person I know who could say no to that would be the guy on the ventilator, who would do it just for a laugh. Then he'd say, "Just smokin' ya, kids. Take all the time in the world."

All the time in the world.

"Are ya just smokin' us, kid?" I ask when we're alone.

All the time in the world. It's not much.

I climb up next to him into the bed, not looking at the

biological version of him but instead the mechanical extensions. I look at the monitors, listen to the respirator. Then I look at the ceiling. I fold my hands.

I can feel him, though. I can feel his temperature, which is warm, and his heartbeat, which is crazy strong—wildly, encouragingly strong.

Except that's my heart. My heart is beating so hard, I think the nurses might come rushing in to respond to it.

"What am I gonna do?" I ask him, because the pathetic truth is I asked him every important question I ever had.

I should not be surprised when I get no answer. But I'm shocked.

"No, Duane," I say, and I roll over onto my side. There's a tube going into his left nostril and tubes coming in and out of his arms and legs, and I may be doing something wrong but I'm careful and I don't care. His head is all bandaged and his neck all braced, and I snuggle up to him like a baby possum clinging to its mother.

When I was three, I killed my Russian dwarf hamster by love-squeezing it to death. The pediatrician told my parents that was common and normal behavior.

I recognize his mouth. That is my brother's smart mouth. He'd just gotten the mustache the way he wanted it, finally. His Manchu was just Fu enough, he said. I lightly trace the corners of his mouth with my thumb and forefinger.

"I know you better than this," I say. "Come on now, man. I know you better than anybody, and I know you better than this."

I wait, again, for him to do what he's always done best. Defy them all.

I wait.

All the time in the world.

I know this is too much, too much time in here in this place of rules and procedures and time-is-of-the-essence. They're giving me far more time than they should.

"I hate you for this," I say, pinching the corners of his mouth a little harder, a little harder.

I have the hiccups as I shove up off the bed, stomp away out of the room, push past my parents and the ICU nurses and all the rest of them. I have the hiccups.

I'm standing with my back to the river's voices again, arms folded, staring up at the window, when my dad approaches. I feel fury as he gets closer, but I see in my peripheral vision that he's not intimidated the way he should be, and he's not breaking stride. My arms are still folded as he reaches me, puts a firm grip on both my biceps, and says the stupidest thing anyone has ever said.

"It's okay now," he says. "It's okay."

It's been a long time since I wanted to hit somebody with malicious intent. Right now my dad feels to me like a gift from God.

As trade-offs go, God, this is a little weak, but at least it's something.

"If you want to take a shot," Dad says, still right there, staring into my eyes.

That shakes me. It's a shaky day.

"If it makes you feel any better, Son, go right ahead. If anything makes you feel better, go right ahead."

Wow. He doesn't hug me or anything, though. Probably figures if he did, I *would* slug him. Probably right.

We stand there, looking I'm sure every which way of weird

to the people strolling by. He holds his grip on my muscles, and I hold my immovable arm-fold, and we stare at each other. A sound eventually comes out of me.

"I have the hiccups," I say.

"I recognize them," he says.

We grip and stare some more. We're both grateful for the river's running commentary.

"We need to go inside, Eric," he says. "We are needed. There is much to do, and some of it is urgent. And while God knows your mother is capable of all of it, he also knows she shouldn't have to be."

I look away from him, and back up to the window, which is only on the second floor but might as well be on a mountaintop.

He gently tugs me where we need to go. I gently allow him to.

"What?" I say when Dad leads me to an office on the floor above Duane's. "What are we doing here when he's down there?"

"Your mother is in here," he says, ushering me in.

Inside I find Ma sitting in a chair with a great fistful of Kleenex like a blue head of cabbage. The main doctor, Dr. Manderson, is sitting next to her in the *comforting* posture I am sure he learned in med school. Wonder if there was a test on it.

"Hello, Eric," says the man whose office it must be, because he comes from behind his teak desk to shake my hand. He greets me with unsmiling warmth as he explains he is David Buick, the unit social worker, and sits me in a chair on the other side of my mother. Dad remains standing by the door. Like the family's strong sentinel, or the one most likely to bolt for the exit.

"Why are we here?" I say, rudely getting to the point.

Just as rudely, though not rudely at all, the point is sent right back to me.

"No," I say expertly now, as "No" is my theme today.

"There is absolutely *no* pressure here," Buick assures me.

"No pressure," Dr. Manderson agrees.

"It is right, Son," Ma says. "It is the right thing . . . the most generous . . ."

"It's what God wants us to do," Dad says.

"What is God's goddamn problem today?" I snap, and pop up out of my chair.

Nobody gasps, or argues with me. Nobody even asks me to calm or sit down. There is no resistance of any kind.

I am left to do it myself.

Pieces of a brother. In somebody else. My brother, my boy.

They were his. His heart, his kidneys.

Good God. His *eyes*.

"No. Hell, no. Hell, no," I say, and storm to the door, and back again.

They were his; now they are mine. That is it, and that is right. No more discussion.

"He never signed a donor card, and he didn't have that thing on his driver's license either," I say pathetically, trumping nothing.

My mother allows herself the tiniest of smiles. "He drove for six months without insurance, too."

I feel instantly better, for an instant, as I remember that and how *Duane* that was. Then the hiccups come thundering back.

"Donor card, my ass." That's what Duane would say right now.

Duane would do it, without hesitation. I half suspect he's downstairs right this minute prying out his own pancreas to give to some kid in Ohio in time for the Babe Ruth baseball season.

Of course he would do it.

"No," I say, and no one in the room buys it.

"Time, Son," Ma says. "Time matters."

All the time in the world.

"And Duane is already gone," Dad adds, "while there are a lot of people who—"

"You should know," I say. "You were dead a long time before Duane."

I don't even mean it. There is nothing wrong with the man or with how he is conducting himself right now. I can only imagine what it all feels like for him, and he's carrying it off with dignity I couldn't dream of. He does not deserve this.

"I'll stop talking if you stop talking, Dad."

It's the best I can do. He answers by not answering.

The most silent minute in the most silent room ever—ends with me turning to my mother, the doctor, Buick, and my dad in turn, and nodding once to each.

Like I have any power at all.

There's a two-seater couch along the wall by the door. I walk over to it and lie down. I curl like a boiled shrimp, and sleep while the rest of them get on with the business of harvesting the rest of the best of my brother.

PIECES

Pieces, Duane called them. His little bits o' wisdom, his small philosophies.

"Here's a piece for ya, boyo," he would say when he was getting all wound up and windy. "Self-awareness is a great thing. Unless you're trying to sleep."

PETE HAUTMAN

SIMON & SCHUSTER | BFYR

TEEN.SimonandSchuster.com